PILOTS OF THE LINE

PILOTS OF THE LINE

Sky Masterson

iUniverse, Inc.
New York Lincoln Shanghai

Pilots of the Line

iUniverse, Inc.

For information address:
iUniverse, Inc.
2021 Pine Lake Road, Suite 100
Lincoln, NE 68512
www.iuniverse.com

This is a work of fiction. While as in all fiction, the literary perceptions and insights are based on experience, all names, characters, places and incidents are either products of the author's imagination or are used fictitiously. No reference to any real person or airline is intended or should be inferred. Many stories presented in this novel have appeared in Airways magazine (Airways International, Inc.), some under different titles.

For more information:
www.skymasterson.com

ISBN: 0-595-31505-4 (pbk)
ISBN: 0-595-66327-3 (cloth)

Printed in the United States of America

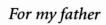

For my father

Certainly any novel requires the effort of more than a single person. Without the support and confidence of John Wegg, and the talented people at Airways magazine, this work may never have seen the light of day. The same appreciation goes to clear eyed editors like Sue-Ellen Gower, and my greatest supporter, confidante, and friend, Karren Madson. Also, I wish to thank those managers, mechanics, and other workers in the airline industry whose often overlooked, sometimes heroic, measures rarely reach the page. What they do is often too far removed for air minded minds like mine to adequately comprehend, and adequately relate.

Mark Garfinkel is responsible for "Moon Jet," the outstanding cover photograph of an Air India Boeing 747-437 slashing the moon one winter night over Boston, 2001.

Contents

Part III   Post Tragedy

Pilots of the Line

I lean back in my chair and adjust the knob on a little radio called an Automatic Direction Finder, an instrument with a small needle that points in the direction of the nearest radio station on Oahu. The needle twiddles back and forth, unsure, unable to home in precisely on the transmitting station, because we are still almost two hundred miles away. I can hear faint music from the station through the static in my headset. It is an old tune, perhaps the same that the Japanese navy pilots might have homed in on fifty years earlier on their mission to bomb Pearl Harbor. I am swept into the past, sharing this timeless moment and feeling an odd kinship with those fellow aviators, regardless of their mission, in the desolate blackness of the sky.

In the darkness of the cockpit, I sit behind Frank and Dusty who fight sleep. Though our day is almost through, we still have another forty minutes to go in our traversing of the southern Pacific Ocean from the west, and the constant hiss of air blasting against us is fodder for our nemesis: fatigue. Each of us is alone with our thoughts. We are quiet within our aluminum jet airplane. That is not to say that there is nothing significant to say, just that there are only a certain number of words that men can pass during sixteen hours. After so much time spent contemplating life on the edge of space, seeing neither ship wake below, nor contrail above, the feeling of insignificance becomes overwhelming to the point of making words meaningless.

We are wanderers who have long forgotten what a home is. This hopping from city to city as we bridge the Pacific Rim, this running from life as we change domiciles and change destinations, becomes a reason for living. The momentum of our movement fuels us, like sharks that die when they stop moving, searching, on the hunt.

We are Pilots of the Line.

PART I

KINSHIP

Concourse E

"Mister, when we get up in the air, can I fly the plane?"

I blinked my eyes hard and turned to find the little boy standing there just behind the center pedestal. He was about seven or eight, had one of those little boy haircuts with the straight bangs, and a blue and yellow striped shirt. His father stood behind him with a small camera as other passengers turned the corner toward their seats.

"Well now, do you think you can handle her?" I asked.

He looked around at the array of dials and switches, knobs and levers, stuck the end of his finger into his mouth and said, "Maybe if you show me?"

I suppressed a laugh. "Have a seat, partner," I said, boosting him up into the vacant captain's seat, and then slid the seat forward.

Now, some children jump right up there into our little sacred domain and immediately grab at the landing gear lever almost quicker than I can guard it, laugh and punch at the throttles as if their destruction would have no ill effect on our safety. Some say not a word, but sit there, unaffected by the wonderment of flight, only to please their overbearing parents. And then some want to really fly.

The fire behind this child's eyes told me that he was drinking in the tidbits of knowledge that I introduced to him about the machine. It wasn't much—a steering wheel of sorts, throttle levers that made us go, the blue and brown attitude indicator that told us which side was up when we couldn't see for the clouds and fog. These things aren't hard to understand. He looked at me.

"Then can I fly it?"

"I wish kid. It'd be the most fun you could ever have, for a while at least. I'm not sure about anyone else in the back of the plane, though."

His father laughed. I put my hat on the kid's head and then dad snapped a picture.

"Sorry, pal. Maybe in a couple of years," I said, tousling his hair as the real captain replaced him.

Maybe in a couple of years. Maybe thirty? Was it that long ago?

Once before, a long time ago, I was here, Chicago, in this worn out sheepskin seat, a seat that has held a thousand men for ten thousand days of pounding wind and sweat soaked hands, and blinding suns beating down on narrow runways. So long ago it was, my thoughts then were so pure and innocent, seeing only the good, the desirable, seeing what flying is—to the untested. It was so long ago. Since then, many times have I held this yoke of a horse of a different sort with the power of another ten thousand more being wrested by the whims of my fingertips. Was it then that I knew what I'd be?

Jerked back through a vortex of intervening years, I am that boy again.

I ran to keep up with him, my dad, especially as he walked briskly through the swarm of rootless people in Chicago O'Hare's Concourse E. Of course, I never walked fast enough then. Though a child's legs flutter beneath him, they never get anywhere fast, especially with magnificent airplanes all around beyond the walls of glass. And they were magnificent. I turned my head for a moment, just a moment, to see them—a DC-8 and 707—as they screamed for my attention with breakaway thrust, and he was gone, and…I was lost in that big old place.

I quickened my pace.

Searching from face to face…

Darting between traveler's legs…

"Dad? Where are you?" I yelped, running by the hot dog vendor with rows of people standing at a bar pushing hot dogs into their mouths and wiping mustard from their lips.

He'll be mad.

I ran by a gate with a blue-suited woman talking on a microphone as people stood in line and trickled through a door. I ran as a robed, bald-headed Hari-Krishna pushed a book into my chest and held out a hand for a donation. A donation! From a child?

I ran as O'Hare's unique mature odor of cigar and salt made my nostrils tingle. I ran over the speckled terrazzo floor, passing the restroom. The odor changed from coffee tinged to mint tinged, to body odor tinged. Adult voices melded into a constant hum of incomprehensible tension and joviality, broken by spasmodic interruptions of PA announcements for people to get messages at white paging telephones, whatever they were.

Then I found him, standing there at the end of the concourse, looking at me as though he'd about lost a sack of twenties. As I approached, my heart raced beneath my heaving chest. He held out his hand. It smelled of cologne and cigarettes, and though he gripped mine with the power of ten me's, it was a soft clench that from that point on in Concourse E never left mine.

Though I never knew if he understood what I felt, that airplanes were the wonderment of it all, the salve of a vexed world, he seemed to always put me in places that nurtured my passion, just as a horticulturist fertilizes his prized rose. This is my garden, O'Hare, on a summer afternoon in 1973.

We waited until the stream of people slowed to a trickle before we walked down the Jetway toward the airplane with the red and blue stripe on her tail. As we neared, I became aware of an odor that would never change…the scent of fabric, and perfume, and coffee, and of faraway places that is ever-present on an airplane. And people smiled. As dad went up and shook the pilot's hand, mumbling a request that I could not hear, the stewardess popped a macadamia nut in her mouth and put her index finger up to her lips, as if jokingly implying that it was our little secret. She proffered me one, my first, which I immediately popped into my mouth. It was the first of many glorious discoveries that day. Then the men beckoned me up.

"Young man, why don't you take a seat right there on the left," said the man in the uniform. "That's right, right up to the control column."

I did so, apprehensively.

The stack of instruments was so high that I could barely see the windows, making me think that windows must not be all that important in an airplane.

"That's the control column in front; you pull to go up and you push to go down. Go ahead there, give her a try."

I did and it was heavy. Pilots must be strong.

"We turn her just like a car, see?"

The massive control wheel on my side moved as he turned his side.

He then explained the simplest of instruments: where the throttles were; that the little *wheel-shaped* lever was for the actual wheels beneath us, but "don't touch it on the ground lest we fall on our belly;" and that the flap lever looked like a little flap. And up above, right over my head, were switches that looked like little lights in clumps of three—the landing lights. Certainly, if a wheel lever looked like a wheel, a flap lever like a flap, lights like lights, and a child knew this as with any toy, I deduced that an airplane was no more than a big child's toy. A toy indeed! To spend one's life playing with such a toy would be the essence of a life well spent.

I hesitated, and then reached up, looking for his approval.

"Go right ahead," he said.

Carefully, I pushed the light switches above my head forward, and stood to see through the especially high windshield, the reflected glows of our landing lights in the gate windows ahead of us.

"I did that?"

"You sure did, boy," he said.

I commanded a function of a jet airliner. My mother couldn't do that, nor could my sisters, or any of my other friends. If I could accomplish this at nine years of age, what then at twenty?

"They'll be landing soon," said the voice of my father, "time to move along so that we'll be there when they arrive."

Reluctantly, I rose from the seat, looking back at the pilot who shared his flight deck with me, and my father thanked him. "He'll make a fine pilot some day, I can tell," he said.

For some reason, the words from the man had more effect on me than words from anybody else. If he could tell, then I had nothing to worry about.

"Thank you," I said, taking one last glance at the cockpit and then followed my father.

Even now, O'Hare Airport is perfumed as it was in 1973, with the exception of the lack of cigar smell by the front entrance. People who live there don't recognize this any more than their own midwestern accent, because one must have been here then and away now, to know what hasn't changed.

Unlike the smell of Los Angeles and the smell of New York's LaGuardia and Newark's Liberty—they all have their own aroma, which isn't unpleasant, even when cigars were prevalent—it is unique, because it is O'Hare, an airport of unfathomable size and excitement and history.

Though no one really pays any attention to the floor, I had to because it was the longest path of white and black terrazzo I have since walked upon, and a child watched the floor a lot when he walked with dad. I noticed immediately then when I returned after thirty years that it had been covered with a jovial blue carpet, as if it was an attempt to snuff my cherished memory.

This is Concourse E. There once was a day when I clung to these very windows in wonderment at all that went on beyond them, the seemingly hundreds of men on little tractors pulling trains of baggage carts willy-nilly and never crashing into each other, the peculiar shaped machines designed to push and empty planes, the planes—so incredible. Ahh, the planes are everywhere, moving through the intricate airport maze and then floating skyward toward oblivion. Such things are extraordinary to a young boy who thinks about what it takes to get from there to here figuratively, into the cockpit. The path is as long as my hidden terrazzo floor.

Now here I am, in the cockpit of a passenger jet, thinking that some things change, but most really don't in this ever-spinning cycle of life.

It is my turn to be that man. This is still the same O'Hare, her age hidden behind a crust of make-up. I turned quickly enough to catch the kid and his father before they disappeared down the aisle.

"Kid," I said.

He turned around with his mussed up, little boy, haircut.

"You'll make a fine pilot one day. I can tell."

Requiem for Innocence

Req'ui'em [Webster] n. 2. A composition (musical) or service commemo-rating the dead.

There are men who are one with the air. They are forever calm, pedestals of understanding, and perpetually intrigued by the ways of the wind. They take nothing for granted in the sky, for there is no room for innocence. They have great conviction, a great pride. For instance, in every landing, they create the perfect transition from air to ground, cherishing every moment airborne to the last instant. And a true aviator, a birdman who has an instinctive connection with the air, is what I hope to one day become.

It is a long road to achieving this stage in an aeronaut's life. It doesn't occur by accident, though it may never occur because of one. Youth, in mind or body, rarely takes the conservative path, believing that in order to be an experienced aviator; one must be able to handle whatever is thrown at us. While young, we pushed ourselves beyond our trained levels of com-petence, recovering awkwardly more than once. But then, we were all young and impetuous. To be a birdman is to know when being conserva-tive is appropriate, to not be persuaded to do that which is not safe, and be stoically comfortable whilst performing our duty.

If our ambition is merely to work in the air, never ascribing to oneness with the zephyr, then we are forever stuck in a stage of insecurity with machine and nature, and never truly connected. But the birdman remem-bers. He has allowed the experiences from his past to guide the decisions in his future, and he knows what his capabilities are. My hope is that we learn and grow, and as aviators, all eventually become birdmen.

There is a moment in every flyer's life that changes him forever. It is the first step in becoming a birdman. It is the moment in which our blissful innocence, while held within the ethers, is dashed by the harsh reality of being partly controlled by Mother Nature. It is a time when we first become aware that we can actually perish horrifically if we do not respect air and machine, if we do not stand by our convictions—steadfastly. It is the time when we learn what our convictions are, and what we are made of.

This is that time, 19 years ago.

Roswell was a sleepy little splatter of dwellings and businesses in southeastern New Mexico. Beneath the stars and the blackness that prevailed around them, among the waves of rock, brush, clumps of sage, and chickweed, lay the old Air Force base just on the edge of town. It hadn't been used by the military in over a decade, decaying quietly among the abandoned homes and buildings that surrounded it. Deep within the distant fields beyond the cracked tarmac, beyond the parked, engine-less DC-3 and accompanying corroded Martin 404, lonely coyotes yipped in the whistling breeze. They were accompanied by a thousand other creatures of the night scurrying in the shadows. A far-off roar, a significant thunder, echoed off misshapen buildings that once housed top-secret weapons of war. It rumbled in rhythmic waves, a summer storm of intense magnitude, gradually getting closer. Somewhere in the breeze a door squeaked on rusted hinges, open only to a vacant hangar, as a rabbit darted through it to perceived safety from beneath an unused maintenance platform.

There were a few lights burning in the homes leading up to the airfield. One out of every ten was inhabited as families gradually reoccupied them, just as hermit crabs occupy discarded seashells. One of the few buildings that showed life near the edge of the tarmac was the new airport terminal. It was built by the city in hopes of taking advantage of the old bomber runways that were more appropriate for a city ten times its size. It was designed in the style of the great southwest, with smooth, sand stucco betraying the nondescript white government architecture surrounding it. A few young employees of the local commuter airline and residents waited patiently for the arrival of their next flight due in from Dallas. The station manager stood outside behind the building, eyeing the distant lightning, while looking intently for the rhythmic strobes of the little commuter airliner. He nervously lit a cigarette.

The earth flattened out through much of the southern half of the state, as the temperate winds of old Mexico flowed gently northward over it, keeping Roswell uncomfortably warm and moist that night. Lightning flashes interrupted the blackness of the sky in distant bursts. Crickets chirped, and somewhere far away, a screaming motorcycle broke the tranquility of the far-off storm as it raced along a desolate country road—a man drunk on speed. Then it abruptly stopped and an uneasy silence returned.

I have flown for a relatively short time, this being my third month since getting hired as a copilot for the commuter airline. Though I felt that my experience up to that point was more than adequate for the job of flying people in small, fourteen passenger, twin-engine airliners, I was learning more every day that I was no more than an empty cup waiting for experience to fill me.

My past was not unique. At seventeen, I earned my license to fly small airplanes. I flew wherever I chose, whenever I could over the state of Colorado, admiring the land for what it was—desolate and treeless. I flew into small airports, sometimes in the middle of the night under sparkling skies. Sometimes I landed twenty times an hour, just for the sake of landing. I flew whatever I could afford which was usually undersized and underpowered. And when the weather deteriorated, I did what most other young aviators did. I grounded myself until the sun returned and the skies softened, beckoning for my return.

Soon, I began teaching others how to fly as was the expected next step in making a career out of flying. People trickled into the airport office and asked about flying lessons. Some of them were older than I, with passing interest; some were younger, looking for a direction in life. A young man, barely my own age, became my protégé, eagerly absorbing my own passion for flying machines. We flew about the state in regular sessions, practicing maneuvers that would one day save our lives—stalling, and steeply banking, correcting for wind, and purposely killing our engine in case it might happen naturally. This we did under azure skies, when the sun blanketed us with warmth and a sense of comfort. And there was nothing I couldn't do when I, as an instructor, had unrelenting control, when I could aim for the airport at my whim the minute the sky refused to cooperate.

But that was the life of a young man who didn't really live by the air. To live, one must fly out of necessity, which takes me to my next step in an aviator's life: as a new copilot for a commuter airline.

This evening, before we left Dallas for Roswell, my captain, a blond-headed, former Air Force flyer only a few years older than I with a passion for cooking, had an embarrassingly loud argument with his wife on a pay-phone. Because of this, we were late closing the door to the airplane and leaving the gate. But it wasn't his fault. As I was later to find out, nothing was ever his fault—it was the fault of ground handlers for closing the door too late, the mechanics for walking too slowly, the agents for being too jovial with people, but never his.

"There is quite a line of weather out there, some three hundred miles long," I said, squinting at the dying sun.

"I know," he replied, "I saw it forming just as well as you on the way down."

I could tell he was still thinking heavily about his conversation with his wife, or maybe something else. He looked out the side window anxiously at nothing in particular as we taxied away from the gate in Dallas, for a man has a lot on his mind when his wife is pregnant, and all that that implies.

In the summer sun, a billowing cloud is a beautiful thing to observe. As you near it in flight, it takes on immeasurable shapes of twisting, giant cauliflowers. You could see many of them form in the early afternoon as far as the eye could see, but by nightfall they matured and joined into an immense line of energy, something only beautiful from afar. From our position short of the runway, the sun was no longer visible, being already below the edge of the horizon. The sky was salmon-purple behind giant, black silhouettes of rising cumuli to the west, our direction home.

Neither of us spoke while holding short for take off. I felt the same anxiety that he felt. I knew that the weather was going to be a factor, so did he. It was one of many days that thunderstorms were predicted along our route of flight, but not so intense as to warrant cancellation. It was like any one of a hundred evenings over west Texas, and we were merely one out of twenty planes headed out there toward them. Even so, there was no way we could have known what was about to happen.

There is a reason why private flyers stayed on the ground, because they don't necessarily have a schedule to keep and can put off their fluttering in the air for another time. Not us. We were living by the air and must, by our wits, find an acceptable route through what seemed to be a rather large storm. That, I knew, was what really concerned us regardless of what he claimed bothered him.

We were cleared for take off.

I yawned though I wasn't tired and I wasn't bored. I yawned because my body needed to subconsciously purge thoughts of dread. He cleared his throat for the same reason, and we became airborne, immediately hitting a wall of wake turbulence. He cussed and jerked the plane abruptly while I sat quietly, because my conviction was still in its infancy, my innocence short lived. We took our heading toward Roswell as the sun drifted slowly into the royal blackness of a panorama of winking stars. Unbeknown to us, the ballooning cumulous clouds ahead acquired oneness as if joining hands across Texas.

Soon, I was struck by the meaning of the silence between the two of us. Though the cockpit was not actually quiet, because the radio was ablaze with chatter, we made business-like comments on the operation of the plane; we did not share real, human thoughts. It wasn't routine. The silence hovered between us like a specter, an invisible omen for things to come. I have grown accustomed to the habit of talking freely with my comrade, mostly about women, because the old adage is true: "When pilots are flying, they talk about women, and when pilots are with women, they talk about flying." But we spoke of neither, because anger has masked the real concern: that my captain could not show indecision; he could not show fear; he could not show lack of knowledge, or, in his mind, the crew falls apart.

Though a sea of blackness surrounded us, strobes of lightning flashes illuminated hundreds of billowing plumes gathering ahead of us. It was a wall of wicked electrical energy, flashing in continuous, random strobes that at any other distance would appear to be a beautiful, sparkling frenzy. It was separated only by narrow chasms of black. The radar scanned with a sweeping green beam across a screen of growing, moderate precipitation. It scanned the Texas night from the depths of Wichita Falls to the very edge of San Angelo. It scanned as only a dumb machine can, revealing only what it saw: a night filled with aerial rattlesnakes and scorpions instead of what any decent non-machine would conjure—lies, any lies of smoothness—I didn't care, would surely have been preferred. The farther we went, the more red crept upon the little screen, but there still were fair-sized openings in the line ahead and we aimed for them.

"There, just a little to the left," I said.

"That's what I'm doing," he spat.

"They build so fast. It wasn't anything like this when we came through a little while ago," I said.

"This is west Texas."

I glanced behind me to see that the nine passengers we carried were quiet, a unified look of concern on their faces echoing my own, all except for a pudgy man who wore glasses just behind me who had a look of interest, like a scientist taking mental notes as if he was about to witness a once in a lifetime event. I cracked a cautious smile.

"Excuse me," he said.

"Yes?"

"I have to ask, but I find this fascinating. Do you mind if I lean forward to watch?"

"If you choose," I said, "but please tighten your seatbelt."

"Thank you. As a school teacher, I can't help but want to relay what I am seeing."

"Very well."

The moment my eyes returned to the front I was thrust into my seat belt. My young captain was already sweating as his hands moved in random gyrations trying to steady the little plane.

"I don't like this," I said.

"Me neither."

"Can't we go around it all?" I said.

"It'd be hundreds of miles out of our way. We haven't the gas; besides, there are plenty of holes in the line. We'll just have to pick our way through," he said, without taking his eyes from the instruments. We took another jolt and I tightened my own belt.

Lubbock had long since drifted behind us, though where it was I couldn't exactly say. We turned away from the first big cell in our path, barely nipping the edges of the worst part of it, only to find another in front of us. To that we went around to the right and then left again, and had done so until we only had a general sense of where we were. I could only say that we were headed in a westerly direction, forgoing true navigating while we concentrated on just rounding the next group of aerial obstructions. It was as if we were running head-on into a line of large defensive tackles in a football game, running for our lives with the ball. Everywhere we turned there was another, and another. We jogged to the right, weaved to the left, and the farther west we went, the more the cells popped up, reaching for us with swiping fists.

We had crossed the point of no return. It would be extremely rough to turn back toward any usable airport, since as soon as we went through a hole in the line it closed up behind us. While ahead we aimed for what appeared to be a large hole, by the time we came to it, the cell on the left and the cell on the right had crept closer together, almost to the point of closing just as we got through.

"Damn, that was close!"

"Hang on!"

The airplane banked wildly to the right, and back to the left again in a gust of vertical wind. He gripped the controls tightly, anger was all over his face, but it was the mask of fear, the mask of a very frightened human being.

I cannot describe the sinking feeling of being caught in the middle of a line of building cumulonimbus in the electrical blackness over west Texas. Such loneliness cannot be compared; the feeling of mortality was over-whelming. There is no one else up there to protect you; no one there to take the plane when you've had enough. Every aspect of living is your own responsibility. What to do? Where to fly? All avenues close their doors to us. First we aimed for the tiniest of holes, but it closed up *before* we got there, then we turned back around toward another hole and *it, too,* closed up on us.

The inevitable occurred. The hole closed without an alternative. We entered.

The roar of hail was deafening.

I could not hear the screams.

Two giant, red blotches from the radar reflected in the schoolteacher's eyeglasses, and that was all I could see of him until the lightning streaked across our windshield, temporarily blinding us all. He gripped the pilot seats so intently that his head was even with our shoulders. All we could do was hang on and hope beyond hope that the torment ceased.

I could not think. I could not clearly see. I could barely make out the artificial horizon dancing in front of me. The captain and I both pulled at the controls. And for a tiny moment I spiritually stood back, as if watching myself from above, and saw a young man fighting for his life in what should have been a routine flight. He was fighting there, in a machine surrounded by lightning flashes and pounding hailstones.

Among the chaos came a song. It was barely audible from somewhere beyond the din. It was the song that every aviator knows, and it floated from my lips as though I sang alone in a room while I righted the aircraft. It seemed as though it was the most appropriate thing to do just then, clearing minds of all but essential thoughts of survival.

> *"Off we go—into the wild blue yonder,*[1]
> *Climbing high—into the sun;*
> *Here they come—zooming to meet our thunder,*
> *At 'em boys—giver 'er the gun!*

I had subconsciously bought another minute of my own agony.

Then, I heard more of the song echo from the lips of my captain-cook. In the pandemonium of riding a bull through severe turbulence, he sang:

> *"Down we dive—spouting our flame from under,*
> *Off with one—helluva roar!"*

And another, the man with the curious eyes who sat so close, so much a part of our crew now, joined in.

> *"We live—in fame*
> *Or go down—in flame, HELL!*
> *Nothing can stop the Army Air Corps!"*

We hung on. That's all we could do, keeping the wings upright through the rage of boiling cauliflower, the cruel electricity, and sang, freeing our mind of desperate thoughts. No more did frightened moans linger in the back as they sat silently listening to the men up front freeing their minds from the mortal bonds of fear.

---

1.   Words and Music by Captain Robert Crawford, ©1939 as the "Army Air Corps Song."; renewed 1977 by the USAF

A blast from above, a blast from below, we rocked and shook by the hand of Mother Nature with the wrath of a petulance I cannot describe. And all we could do was hold on and sing.

> *"Minds of men—fashioned a crate of thunder,*
> *Sent it high—into the blue;*
> *Hands of men-blasted the world asunder;*
> *How they lived—God only knew!"*

And, after what felt like an eternity, we burst out the backside of the storm, no longer facing evil blotches of storm clouds, no longer being shaken to our bones, and we became…engulfed in a

tranquil…

night…

sky…

To be one with the air.

We were like children at first, needing an occasional scolding for the mistakes we made, but we learned, as I hope to have. The man who sits assuredly in the left seat of an airliner, an old man with wrinkles who gently corrects the young airman with a twinkle in his eye, the man who feels for the earth with gentle caresses as he departs…or lands, has earned the rank of birdman. And, as all birdmen, he never needs scolding by Mother Nature anymore, because he has lost his innocent ignorance of the air.

Behind Closed Doors

Her emerald eyes won't blink, as the city lights in a yellow haze against the blackness of Louisiana, drift below her side of the cockpit. A strand of car lights trickle across Lake Pontchartrain to the crescent-shaped lights underneath the left seat, my side of the turboprop, and I am captivated in disbelief at what hovers before us. We are both speechless, as the engines inhale, unconcerned.

The orange phantom gradually invades our cockpit. Katy's chocolate hair, now a faint amber, lies gently upon her neck, and the rest of the cockpit glows amber along with it. I am not afraid, nor is she as she shoots a furrowed brow at me, for there is no other person that I would rather experience this with tonight than her, I think. We are sharing this significant occurrence, one that transcends a mere physical encounter, far more than two people could ever expect to share, and it is…unexplainable. And it is…with her. What would I say or do had it been with just anybody else? Would we have scoffed and placed some earthly explanation on it, as men do, and snapped open approved reading materials hoping it would disappear moments later…this apparition, existing only to be spoken about behind a half empty bottle of gin in the hotel bar?

Katy danced in my heart the moment I met her, this seeming Barbie Doll toting a flight bag down the hall, wearing a black pilot hat two sizes too large for her womanly curls. Her feet brushed the floor as she walked, gliding effortlessly, pulling my, and my associates eyes along. I may not have noticed the smile, which never left her face, as I searched her form for imperfections. But when she said my name, asking if I were her captain this day, I couldn't then pull my gaze from it except to look into her soul through her alluring eyes. And they lingered on mine, at least as I would believe.

I first couldn't understand why this woman strolling so nonchalantly toward the weather desk, beaming, could be without some glistening diamond on her hand. There must have been a thousand guys before me who approached her just this year alone, and I imagine she sent the boys packing, telling them to come back only after they became real men. She must on some level be a witch of a woman, not the friendly, sweet, girl before me. She must be.

Twenty years ago, this never would have happened. Women were scarce in the cockpit unless they were bringing coffee and asking what time we would be arriving, and even then it was only when we had our manipulative little blue light turned off. Now we must deal with the demons of our masculinity; accept that this petite woman of thirty or so can manage the bull we call an airplane, this beast we sometimes strut away from like a bow legged cowboy as we pat ourselves on our backs. Now, not only must we work directly with such splendor, but be forced to admit that she, and any woman, can do the job fine, bull or no bull. We must accept that we are not great egotistical cowboys, but the *mere* men everyone else knew we were but us.

We sail high in the night sky at 21,000 feet. The airplane is sturdy and strong. She is fast for her shape and limited horsepower due in part to her thin, highly engineered wing, a wing designed to sponge a maximum amount of lift with a minimum amount of drag on a perfect day. I think these wings are a bit underengineered for an imperfect day, however, but I don't get paid to question physics. I do get paid to ride the designer's philosophy, perfect day or not. Its tail is neither something I wish to contemplate nor ridicule, because there isn't enough of it there for me to comfortably tease. The engine gauges are rock steady; they know no difference between razor sharp skies and ambiguous formations ahead. They purr ignorantly, because they are inorganic, which is fine. I trust them all, wings, tail and engines regardless of their imperfections, because they work in unison, reliably, thankfully, so that Katy and I can concentrate on this oddity, instead of on them misbehaving.

I have never seen, in my years of flying commercially, such a sight—this giant floating square above New Orleans. It is so perfect, so unnatural, because its sharp, straight corners are nonexistent other than among man's creations. I have no explanation. Yet it hovers, unmoving, and I—*we* are awestruck. Could it be the beginning of Armageddon? The sign that we humans have messed up what we could on this earth and the end is near? Is this specter the inheritor of our oft-abused earth, and coming to correct us? Will it grow and take over the entire sky before it sucks New Orleans below and then the rest of the world, in some slow, gloomy ooze?

Maybe this impossible alien sees our achievements and has come to praise us on our accomplishment of spreading love and peace to all mankind. Maybe this is as close to peace as any alien scientists thought we could achieve and we pass, their experiment now being over. Maybe there are no more fascists and tyrants to challenge us since we have survived all that they could dream of sending us. They are happily ready to take us all back now, back to the mother ship, and plant us on another fuzzy rock in space to see how we develop there. Maybe we will do better; maybe we won't last as long. Is it *they* who have come? We face it directly, flying through the air at two hundred and ten knots, yet we never seem to get closer. How is this so?

I don't risk an announcement for fear of pandemonium in the back, but I check my annunciator panel, ensuring that my question hits the proper ears, and finger the cold transmit button on my control wheel for a moment. The air between the speakers in my headset is quiet. I push the tiny green microphone hinged to the side of my left earmuff next to my lips and break radio silence.

"Houston, got time for a question?"

The voice between my ears immediately speaks as if it was waiting impatiently by its own microphone.

"Go ahead," it replies in a loud Texas drawl.

"Anyone report any unusual sightings tonight?"

It is silent for a moment. "No, can't say that I've heard of any," is its response. "You see something?" it adds.

"No," I lie. "Thank you." I release the switch.

The top left side of my head itches as it does when I am confused, and I scratch it until it subsides. I look below to the side of the specter, then over the top, hoping to see some flashing strobes or anything that would suspend it, if something so large can even be suspended, but I see nothing. And as if compelled to check every possibility, I sniff deeply, noting no exceptional odor. I smell airplane, the ever-present sweetness of upholstery and aluminum and heated wires and old food, a touch of glycol, and, of course, the jasmine soap Katy used earlier in the day—an airplane.

Silently, we sit and ponder.

As I scratch my head again, I can't help but think that our pilot lives are not like any other. I know we are the lucky chosen few to not have to sit between four walls everyday, and never see anything new for an entire career. But we are, on occasions like this, challenged by something that causes us to question our very reason for existence. And though sometimes I think it would be nice to feel safe in my sturdy, tiltback, Olefin office chair all day, I wonder if life would be truly worth living without an occasional challenge for life itself. Maybe that's why people bungee jump off bridges, parachute off cliffs, walk on hot coals, and we are aloft here in a mere machine, a man-made machine. It is the risk of not always being certain that makes living worthwhile.

Neither of us fears this thing. Katy doesn't sweat. She doesn't shake in fear. I guess I mustn't, either. Pilots don't generally fear something because it is merely unknown. She is an example of that. We are often curious to learn why something is or isn't so, for example, why the control wheel sometimes is very stiff and sometimes very loose. Could it be that there is a kink in the cable? Or is it merely because the hydraulics are stiff and cold first thing in the morning? Maybe it's just in my head. It makes sense to question rather than panic.

She clears her throat sweetly, looks over at me and lifts a questioning shoulder.

"The face of God," is all I say.

She brings her hand to her scalp and rakes a curl from her vision. "No."

So assuredly, I think. Why not? How can you so knowingly say that it isn't?

"How do you know?" I say.

"Because only wackos believe in God."

Suddenly, I feel the beauty of her form begin to disappear before my eyes. I want to argue, but understand that though we share a love of aviation, we don't necessarily share all beliefs.

Rather than push the issue, I sit quietly in my seat and finger the condition levers so that the propellers are perfectly synced.

The intercom chimes from the back.

"Yes," I say.

"Captain, may I come up there?" our young flight attendant asks. Normally, she isn't so formal. Normally, she doesn't sound so concerned. I wonder how she will react to what we see. Will she scream? Will she cry?

"Of course."

A few seconds later, I hear her unlock the cabin door beyond the baggage pit that separates the cockpit from the passenger cabin. I hear her walk on her thin, black soles across the aluminum pit flooring. Without looking back, I feel her presence between us.

"I have extra turkey sandwiches from the back. Would you care for some?" she asks.

No scream?

"Oh my, look at that beautiful moon," she says.

"Moon?"

"The way the setting orange sun reflects upon it, and the way the clouds frame it like a perfect square. You are so lucky to see such a beautiful sight," she says.

As we continue across the sky with nary a nudge of turbulence, living momentarily in the tube we sometimes curse as, "The Plastic Pig," gradually the clouds that made perfect square edges framing the moon, part in wisps of jellyfish tendrils. The moon. It mocks me like a big, shining Jack-O-Lantern.

"No, thanks," I say, and Katy shakes her head no to the food.

"It sure is neat," the flight attendant says, and departs to serve another person in the back.

Alone, and in the darkness we sit, Katy and I.

The engines inhale unconcerned, still.

It is indeed beautiful, more so because my partner has enough respect for me to not say, "I told you so."

Our Love of Flight is but a Thorny Rose

A wicked specter floats among us as we drone through the night sky. There is a choppiness that inhabits the mountain air, and we lurch as we carry our load of wintertime skiers. I have flown this route a hundred times this year: Boulder; Granby; the Gore Range; over a thousand alluring crevasses for mountain loving beings. The Continental Divide lies forty minutes behind, below the thick stratus layer that tickles the earth and extends to someplace we'll not see, but the beauty of the Rockies is not my fascination tonight.

Something lurks beyond our realm. I clear my throat and the interruption makes Don, my sturdy copilot, jump like a cat under a rocker. I am not alone in my assessment. I click between eight DC and AC generators—volts, amps, all normal. Engine gauges steady. He looks in the blackness for only a second then focuses abnormally long on his flight gauges. Everything is normal, yet nothing is, and I can't quite place my finger on it.

Don tunes in the ADF receivers and for the duration of our approach, I will listen to the constant scratchy identifying tone beeping annoyingly in my ears. In the event we should lose the signal for the microwave due to snow piling up on the antennae, we will have our ancient ADF as our only back up to fly the approach through the mountains around Steamboat Springs. The needles creep back and forth in the marginal radio reception in the Rockies, never resting on a particular bearing to the station, and we can really only guess our position by them, which is a hell of a way around granite.

Don flicks the synchrophaser off, the propellers begin their audible waddle, and he gradually pushes the condition levers forward. Our four rumbling propellers whine, like weary Clydesdales, huffing along the wing, protesting the inconsiderate spurring of their ribcages. With each inch of forward movement of the levers, I can feel the increasing drag from the propellers digging in like pie plates and airspeed lags. I tweak the throttles and the airplane devours into the blackness. And we begin the microwave approach just abeam Rabbit Ears Pass.

"Have them run out and brush off the TALAR antennae," I say, "Don't want them to do it too soon or the snow will pile up again; too late's no good, either."

"Right on it," Don replies.

"Gear down."

Don reaches for the wheel-shaped handle and throws it down while talking on the radio to Steamboat operations. The nose wheel pops out and makes a sound of a baseball bat hitting the hood of a car, as it naturally does, and the wind hisses more loudly at our feet. She sways barely detectably as first the left main gear locks, and in an instant, the right. Three green lights—good.

"Landing checklist."

He obediently takes the card from the holder and mumbles robotically through it. My replies are well rehearsed.

"Flaps forty-five."

"Flaps forty-five."

Her nose pitches down and I roll the trim wheel by my right leg a quarter turn. All we have to do now is land.

Below us, snow drifts along the icy Yampa River that wanders through the valley like a discarded Christmas ribbon. Great ranches with rotting barbed wire fences frame the rolling hills in a white patchwork quilt. To the right, the last of the evening skiers have long shushed their last mogul on Steamboat Mountain, and I imagine them sitting lazily on fat chairs in the lodge, barely noticing our four Pratt engines plying what they hope is tomorrow's heavenly powder.

Don is wet behind the ears, but boasts a seasoned assuredness in his twenty-four-year-old brain. Had I not known he was a year on line, I would have guessed him to be an old salt, never needing prodding to stay ahead of the airplane, setting my side up as well as his own, keeping me out of the dirt. Anymore, a year is an eternity in the commuter airline business, yet only time can teach the foibles and idiosyncrasies of flying through mountain air masses and over jagged rocks. One's hair grays soon, or falls out doing this and his is full and black…but maybe in another year.

I follow the blue and brown attitude indicator, my only reference to the horizon, as we drift down the glideslope. The microwave needles move in micrometers, displaying the steep approach, moving toward a perfect "+." The instruments jitter with increased sensitivity the nearer we get to Steamboat, and I tap the pedals by my feet ever so gently to keep them centered. I scan the left; I scan the right. Don's eyes shoot laser beams into his side of the panel.

"Two thousand feet," he says.

"Set in the missed approach altitude."

"It's there."

"Thank you."

I rub my wet palm on my leg, and then switch hands.

"See anything?"

"Nope."

The farther down we go I quash more fear. The snow is deep, the runway is short, the night is dark, and that phantom drifts among us. Blackness is all around. The airspeed quivers, but resumes its grudging slowness. She's like a truck, so heavy and slow. The wheel is rubber and my seat is full of eggshells. Bank a little left.

"Winds?" I ask.

"Down the runway. A thousand feet to go."

Speed good; vertical good, too. If we miss the approach, it will be straight ahead and then left off the ADF, back toward Hayden and then Buffalo Pass toward home. No need to push the weather.

"Coming up on minimums."

Engines sound funny.

Attitude perfect. It doesn't feel right, g-forces, strange.

Needles crisscross, and then diverge as if pulled by magnets.

"Where are you g-?" he says.

"What?"

In an uncontrolled response, his diaphragm pulls cold air through his partly opened mouth and into his lungs, as if filling them would turn his body into a bouncing beach ball. His gasp never ends; it just starts, and in the course of two seconds, I stop hearing anything.

Most of my instruments—airspeed, altitude, course arrows—suddenly spin fatally, betraying my wholesome attitude indicator. Though it lasted a second, my perplexity is the culmination of a thousand nightmares. It bore into me forever. Why are they doing that?

In that second of deception, our airplane rolls over on her back, and we hit the mountain with a deadly blast.

The party was over. We now received the life of a statistic.

Am I angry? No, there's an eternity for anger. Fear is saved for the living; I am not afraid. I have opened the crypt door and walked through, seen what many great aviators have seen, but few related. I have been discombobulated in a way that no training has ever prepared me for, just like the saying goes: "It's what's not trained for that kills you," and I have never seen this before. The world goes black. The machine ceases to run. There is no sound.

"Do you know what happened?"

The voice broke the silence as if God pierced the heavens, questioning my greatest sin. I look at Don. He is still in one piece, but just as silent as the simulator. I am overwhelmed with bewilderment, for I have never died and had to critique my performance before.

I sit, silent.

"I failed your attitude gyro," says the simulator training instructor sitting behind us.

Ah, yes, the attitude gyro. That explains why our world looked so perfect right down to the crash. As the gyro imperceptibly spun down, I made unnoticeable corrections believing I was maintaining wings level when it cheated me and rolled us dismally. The attitude gyro, a pilot's favorite instrument, because it makes us think we can see through clouds, was the only one *not* working properly, which is why all the others seemed to react strangely in the last moment. I thought it was *they* who betrayed me, not my favored attitude indicator.

"But there was no red flag, no caution light," I protest.

"You only have a flag with a power source failure. I just failed the gyro itself. You always had power to it," says the instructor.

As I look across the instrument panel, I am painfully aware that our particular plane has no standby attitude indicator. A cross check of one would perhaps have saved us on this occasion. Don's indicator worked fine, though. But with only two attitude indicators, and no system to compare them telling you when one has failed, whose do you believe? Don was my only source for discrepancy information, other than my own cross panel check. He looked as perplexed and deflated as I.

"Something was wrong in those few seconds. I wasn't sure whose attitude indicator was wrong, just that something was wrong. It was only a few seconds!" Don sprang up.

"That's all you had," the instructor replies.

"Well, that's bullshit!" I said, "You don't fail a guy's attitude indicator so close to the ground like that. The human brain can react only so fast."

"True," he says, "life can be unfair."

I can feel my body temperature begin to rise as a bead of sweat trickles down the back side of my neck and disappears in the mush of my wet back. The simulator seems extremely warm. I am angry. I am angry at myself for my inadequacies as a pilot.

"I wanted to prove a point," he says. "Every once in a while we come across a scenario that uncovers a fault in our accepted beliefs in operating our airplanes. No airplane is perfect so we must adapt our thinking for every possible known situation that can occur. You must be diligent in recognizing a failure of any instrument at any moment," he says.

My death is still my main concern.

"So be it," I say.

"The rest of your ride went just fine. I just wanted to show you this scenario with the extra time we had."

Thank you, I think, for showing me life's fragility, for opening my naive eyes to the ugliness of reality. I am still dead and will forever miss the blissful innocence of those who know only what it is to live.

Nightmares are not cruel things. They allow us to experience our greatest fears while we subconsciously control the outcome. Then we wake, our minds being cleansed of evil thoughts as in a confessional, as we clear space for the trickling in of more evilness to inhabit.

The simulator is not a nightmare. It is very real. If I pinch myself in it, it hurts. Thousands of people have gone through great strides to create realism so believable that the men who fly them sweat real perspiration, and hearts beat, at times, exceedingly fast. And the simulator's worth as a tool is immeasurable in training pilots to react successfully to scenarios that otherwise only dead men know. But with each maneuver, a tiny piece of simulation becomes reality for the pilot. Maybe no real engine has failed under his command, but he has heroically saved the plane from hundreds of catastrophes in his mind via the virtual reality of the simulator. The pilot's boosted ego is real; his confidence is real. Should he experience a simulated death, it also takes on a magnified eternal life in the deep recesses of his brain.

An airplane is not forgiving. It is not perfect, nor is it ever perfectly operated. It is a big, beautiful animal, one that bites as well as licks and purrs. It is a thing to respect, because mere novices become only statistical fodder, mangled in a joke of pathetic incompetence. A pilot learns through the simulator that an airplane deserves nothing less than supreme respect by never leaving one's guard down, never trusting that all is well, never trusting that all its needs are met, because they never will be. And, like a phantom in the dark it will take all that he holds dear, not because it is programmed to, but because it is only human to become complacent when all is perceived to be well.

Why are these airplanes, their elegantly sculpted wings and engines and tails, so beautiful to us? Is it that they can take us far from our troubles, to the most exotic places we can imagine? Is it because they allow us to experience freedom in ways that Man, until a century ago, was never able to achieve? Why do our eyes well up with water when we see the *chopper* split the body of an old hulk in two?

We have not mastered them at all, but, in fact, *they* have mastered us. They show us that we are human when they fill us with joy on the perfect morning climbout, as we pierce the scattered layer on our quest for paradise.

So when I see my beautiful airplane, her wings still firmly attached by their roots to her unblemished body; her engines still strong, unstrewn about Steamboat Springs, I don't see a mere machine. I don't see a vehicle devised for the sole purpose of transporting masses to locations over the horizon. I see my teacher when I carelessly forgot to flip a switch, my lover who strokes my fragile ego by allowing me to ease her onto the earth in a driving rain, and sometimes the vehicle of my most prodigious nightmares.

The Companion

The Pacific Ocean is a lonely place in the middle of the night. The moon, glistening in the black lacquer sea below, mocks we weary airmen between finger-like clouds. We are a speck in the sky, a speck of life floating within infinite nothingness, and there is an overwhelming sense of our insignificance in the air. We are newcomers to this ocean, which has survived a million times our lifespan. And already, as our contrail drifts and dissipates ten miles behind us, and the rumble from our 727's JT8D-9 engines fades into the inaudible surf below, we disappear specter-like along with them, further into this abyss as though we were never here.

Being a flight engineer is not as glamorous as being a flying pilot. As pilots actually hold the airplane in their hands, fondle her by strokes of the control wheel, feel her vibrations through rudder pedals and a cluster of throttles, I sit at a small desk and sometimes look at gauges. The two ahead of me are content looking out their own windows and making things called decisions. Pretty girls even talk to them. But they understand engineers, because many professional pilots have been engineers at some time in their lives. So they thoughtfully include us in on most decisions. Some considerate pilots even offer us the first choice of crew meals. They understand that the bulk of our professional life consists of taking requests from the cabin crew to turn up the temperature every hour, which consists of gently twisting a black, horned knob a few microns. So, I grant them respect by always choosing the stuffed cabbage over the steak, and reverently accomplishing whatever task they ask of me, because I know that if I am lucky, then one day, I too, will have an engineer of my own to feel sorry for and work like a cabin boy.

After the first hour of flying out over the Pacific, conversations lag, all the best stories had already been told, and silence follows an uneasy transition. Maybe for a while one of us reads something "approved," maybe at another time one of us unbuckles his safety belt and walks to the back to fumble through the galley for a stale dinner roll. Instead of a continuous thread connecting us together as a team, we are severed through boredom into unique beings and, though we are only a few feet apart for long hours at a time, we are in our own worlds contemplating our own thoughts. Perhaps one of us thinks about a parent who died a decade earlier, fondly remembering his first driving lesson with them as he sips coffee. Perhaps the other just remembered that he forgot to take out the trash before he left for his trip. Perhaps no one is thinking about anything at all.

The cockpit is quiet except for the sound of air streaming persistently against our windows and the occasional turning of a page. We are over 5000 miles from the nearest air traffic controller in Oakland, and they can't talk to us directly if they wanted to, so our position is relayed to them by a radio relay station in Honolulu, people who relay rather than control, by using the HF radio. The HF radio has the range to cover half the earth depending on the position of the sun, but the downside is that the communication is often filled with static and stray beeps and garbled words. To listen to this mess for long would push one to insanity. So, the cockpit is void of extraneous radio chatter, because when we don't need to give a position, the volume of our radio is turned all the way down and it becomes a very isolated place.

As minutes drag into hours, I note the time we passed Fiji and begin to plot our position on a map with a pencil.

Angela has been working her radio relay job since midnight and is on her third cup of coffee. The dimly lit room is a familiar place and she is comforted by the lack of fluorescent light, which makes her feel more beautiful than she really is. She likes her job as a radio operator, though she wishes there was more to it than relaying messages from far away men in airplanes to decision makers in Oakland, and feels that it would be nice to use her education in marketing more fully one day. Sometimes the nights drag on like an endless road facing a truck driver, but she rarely complains, because she knows it is difficult to find a job that lets her work through the night on the island of Oahu and relax there during the day. In the morning after work, she often naps on a blanket on Kaneohe beach underneath the shade of coconut palms swaying in the cool, Pacific air.

She has contemplated a large map on the wall in front of her thirty-two times in the last hour, trying to mentally equate the position of her airplanes with the coordinates that the pilots read to her. Four men do the same at workstations within the room, but they are separated by sound-proof half-walls and are too far away from her to carry on a decent conversation. Though she wears a headset, the extraneous sounds of mumbling voices infiltrate her thoughts and she finds it difficult to daydream about lying on the beach when she isn't there. She adjusts the volume knob on her radio display and wonders what kind of an accent her next caller will have. Will he be a Japan Air-liner? Philippine Airways? Maybe Qantas from down under?

I turn the volume up on the number one HF radio. Renegade pings and beeps play among the static of the high frequency from the speaker in our cockpit. Occasionally, distant voices lost in the fuzz of radio space speak broken English in odd accents to far away relay stations. It is as though I am listening to aliens communicate, their voices bending in unnatural ways along the wide, invisible radio waves. Someone with a French accent says, "Air France is ready to report position." Someone else who sounds Japanese says, "Japan Air will repeat." I listen to the sounds while looking at the onyx beyond the windows. There is life outside my window, I know, regardless of the isolation I feel…life all around us separated by thousands of miles…floating from the speaker above and my headset. The two ahead of me perk at the tangled sounds, but remain solidly engaged in their thoughts as I accomplish this task.

I pull my microphone from its bracket and note that although most of the other aspects of this airplane have kept up with modern design, the microphone somehow looks as though it would be more appropriate in an old bi-wing bomber from World War One. It is round and battered and dangles from a twisted wire off a broken mount. Clearly fidgety engineers, with wayfaring thoughts, have abused it over the years regardless of the comfort it brings. As I key it, I find out too late that my volume is turned up too high again, and I forgot to channelize. None of the other radios need to be channelized before making a transmission besides the HF, which is why it is an easy thing to forget. A loud tone screeches into my ears for four seconds, momentarily stabbing my ear with pain. The two men in front of me jump in their seats; tossing annoying looks in my direction, then turn back to their thoughts. I then hear an operator from Tokyo drift between pops of static, and Manila, too. I wait impatiently as though I am trying to merge onto a busy highway with an underpowered car.

In a break between frenzied chatter, I make my stand. I call, "Honolulu, Honolulu, Forty-One Golf Echo, position."

There is static. I hear a stray tag of Morse code, or conflicting radio signals that create beeping patterns sounding the same, but no response. I check my watch. I wonder if I might possibly have the wrong frequency, if perhaps someone tried to call us with a change and I missed it. In the back of my mind, as deep into the blackness of the Pacific as we are, I even wonder if Honolulu is still there at all or if it somehow sank into the sea.

"Honolulu, Honolulu, Forty-One Golf Echo, position," I say again with a little more desperation.

"Forty-One Golf Echo, this is Honolulu, go ahead with your position," says Angela. Her voice is more articulate than the rest. It is soft and comforting and feminine and assured. But there is something there, the inflection in the way she said, "this is Honolulu," was as if she was trying to say more, like the captured spy who blinked "S.O.S." into the camera. I envision her alone like me, sitting in the near darkness, surrounded by people who are their own islands in a sea of nothingness. It is as though she just walked into the cockpit and sat next to me, speaking with a wavy resonance caused by the wide radio waves of the HF transmission, a beautiful alien, my friend in nothingness.

"Forty-One Golf Echo, position," I said, "North One Six Zero Eight Two, East One Three Seven Four Niner Three. Fuel remaining: twenty-eight decimal zero. Next position Mike-Alpha-Delta-Sierra."

Silence returns except for a few crackles. I did all that I could to relate my gratitude at finding her through inflection and the tone of my report, just as I perceived her thoughts, but did she understand that I understood? It was my own blinked "S.O.S."

"Roger, Forty-One Golf Echo," she replies, "I received your position, I received your position," she inexplicably repeats, "Stand by for a SELCAL (SELective CALling system) check,"

I wait impatiently like a suitor waiting for the phone to ring. Then at once came a tone as if someone had pressed the digits on a touch-tone phone three times, and a *ding-dong* chimes like a doorbell in the cockpit. This seemingly insignificant check, which is the same that she gives to every other pilot, felt like a special gift just for me. The joy I feel cannot be described. Someplace, an almost unfathomable number of miles across the ocean, there is a lonely woman reaching out for a companion. She pitched from a mound over five thousand miles away, and I swung.

"SELCAL check okay for Forty-One Golf Echo," I reply, trying as much to sound like what a famous, good looking, Hollywood actor might sound.

"Honolulu, roger," she says, and static returns again after her inflection rose as if she meant to say more. She drifts away, as I do from her radio, and our lives begin to diverge as they all do, back into loneliness, lives void of meaning.

"Honolulu," I say.

"This is Honolulu!" she quickly responds.

I want to see her. I want to bring her into my world. She is special, my companion in the night. I want to learn all about her, share a lifetime of the joy she brings to me as she has tonight over this dark, empty ocean. But how? The long reaching arms of the HF meant that hundreds of curious ears could hear our every transmission.

"Good night, Honolulu," I say.

"Good night, Forty-One Golf Echo," she replies.

Static dominates my headset and the cockpit speaker again. Her voice is gone and again we are alone like islands in a sea of humanity. I put my pencil and map down on the small table in front of me. The copilot makes a muffled cough into a clenched fist. For the first time, I notice that all three of us gaze into the blackness through the windows. Am I wrong to think that they envy me at being the one to actually talk to our companion?

Specks of starlight twinkle in the sea below us, and the night ahead. The air is without ripples. Someone turns a page.

The North Platte Incident

Imagine for a moment that you are her. Fifteen years later, would you still be thinking about it, still cringing inside instead of sitting smugly in your comfortable chair with nary a care in the world? Would it still be on your mind after all these years? I think about it occasionally, what it must have been like back there, sitting there in quiet mortification between and among the others. Yet, my life is none the worse because of it. In fact, in an unwholesome sort of way, I have gained a little notoriety from it. I am known as the guy who…But, I'm getting a little ahead of myself. It began in an airplane, as it always seems to.

You hardly see any *C* model Beechcraft 1900's anymore. If you see any at all, they are usually the *D* models, the one with the higher cabin ceiling, the airplane with the nickname, *Flipper*, because it's the little commuter airplane with the hump back and the pointy snout and the mess of stabilons, tailets and vortex generators that I'll just call *fins* on her tail. The *C* model is a prodigy of the Super King Air, which is the evolution of hundreds of successful aircraft made by the Beechcraft Corporation over the years. It is the first pressurized, nineteen-passenger, twin engine commuter aircraft produced by Beech for entry into that particular market in the United States, and was in many ways better than other aircraft of similar size made by other manufacturers.

It is a pilot's airplane. Like most Beechcraft, it is perceived as stable and durably made. It has a certain ruggedness about it as though it was designed more for hard landings in the bush instead of well maintained city airport runways. And with the reliable, twin 1100 horsepower Pratt and Whitney engines, it was thought to easily out climb most similarly sized aircraft such as the Swearingen Metroliner 2, and BAE Jetstream 31, and could carry more weight, with better single engine performance at high altitude airports. It handles well in the roughest winds. All in all a delightful aircraft to fly with only a few minor drawbacks common to most other commuter aircraft of the size, being: a cramped cockpit; no autopilot; no flight attendant and no lavatory.

The cabin is long and narrow and intimate. Each seat is both an aisle and a window seat with the exception of the last row, nine rows back, which has three abreast seating along the aft bulkhead. Because the cabin is so cigar tube-like, it gives one the feeling of claustrophobia, especially those sitting in the aft seat. If the sliding cockpit doors happen to be open, the passengers in the far back of the plane could see up through the forward windshield, resulting in airsickness from the optical illusion of the aircraft swinging wildly down along the approach to the runway. Often these sliding doors were left closed for that very reason, though there is no regulation that states an aircraft of this size requires them to be.

There is no place that better epitomizes the heart of small town America than North Platte, Nebraska; a place where, unbeknownst to me, my education in the amount of ignominy a human can withstand began. North Platte is situated near the center of a state that is in the center of this country. "It is the place where everything that's good happens," the locals like to think, where most types of injustice are unknown to most people. Old folks outnumber the younger who have left for more excitement elsewhere, but they'll return, as they often do, to live among the values that are often swept away in the big city like cigarette butts in front of a skyscraper. Generations of farmers there scratched an existence in the earth since the days following Horace Greeley's famed proclamation: "Go west, young man." To which, those who understood the value of lush prairie went no farther than this fertile Platte Valley. Though it has since been home to the famed "Buffalo Bill," it also, and more appropriately, should be known as the home of Jack Knight, pilot of the first night segment of the first transcontinental airmail route flown through blinding snow. And like Jack, the current residents of North Platte are very prideful, modest, and decent.

We checked in for the trip, my first officer, Red, and I, after a short van ride down Philip Avenue. He was my comrade that day, because of an experimental pilot program that allowed fresh college graduates to fly as flight engineers on larger jets at a subsidiary company for a year or two before coming down the ranks to fly as a copilot in my smaller sized aircraft. Officially, he was more senior than I, but because his flying time was limited, I was, in essence, his instructor and captain. Because he had flown as a crewmember on a larger jet, he brought with him a professionalism that was rare for low time copilots of little nineteen passenger airplanes. Young captains loved flying with guys like Red. Not only was he meticulous beyond what we were used to, but also his confidence brought forth such a relaxed atmosphere in the cockpit that any aspect of flying with him was nothing less than a joy.

The Beechcraft sat like an enormous, lifeless, Nebraska crow beyond the back door of the operations room. The dawn sun was still just below the horizon, and the sky was a pallid black with signs of florescent life in the distant east. Though there was a chill in the air, the sight of an airplane pending flight on a crisp morning, unleashed a certain enthusiasm known only to prideful pilots. I pulled myself up the airstair and flipped on the master switch thereby giving life to the machine. I then returned to the ramp, it being my duty to walk around the plane, a duty that in most cases was delegated to the copilot, but in this case he had the more mundane task to accomplish of loading bags from a cart parked abeam the large aft cargo bin. Once finished, he stood in front of the forward entryway and assisted passengers up the narrow stairs into the cabin while I returned to the cockpit and scribbled numbers on the load manifest.

One by one they entered, mostly businessmen on their way to a meeting in Denver or cities west. They climbed up the airstair, hunching their backs as they turned the corner into the cabin, some of them hanging a coat in the tiny coat closet just behind the pilot seats, and then found their own. When the trickle of people finally ended and the last one found his seat somewhere behind me, Red climbed the steps two at a time as he had done so hundreds of times before and pulled the door closed. He crouched as he turned the handle and checked it for security.

"Did you miss me, boss?" he said with a hint of a Chicago accent, as he slipped into his tiny side of the cockpit.

"Not particularly," I joked, and handed him a small brown bag and a cup of coffee.

"What's this?"

"I stopped by the snack bar and got us a couple of éclairs and coffee while you stood out there smashing bags into the cargo compartment. Creamer's in the bag. I didn't know if you take it that way or not."

"Thanks, you're not such a bad guy no matter what everybody else says about you."

"When you're ready, we're clear on two."

"Spin it," he said, and we ran through the checklist.

I engaged the starter. Immediately the igniter on the number two engine on the right side of the airplane began to "tick." The propeller slowly began to turn. At the minimum engine rpm, I pushed the condition lever forward thereby adding fuel and, with a small burst of flame, the engine came to life.

"The engine has stabilized," he said.

I made the gesture for them to pull the ground power with my fingers.

Out of the corner of my eye, I saw an agent hustling toward the airplane with a woman who was pretty, wearing a bright orange dress.

"Looks like we've got a straggler. Could you let her in?" I said.

"Sure," he said, unfastening his seatbelt and then removed himself from his seat to unlock the cabin door. Our engine noise was magnified throughout the cabin.

"Hurry up," I thought. No need to have people near the airplane with the propeller spinning even if it was on the opposite side. But in a moment, he closed the door again. I wasn't the only one who liked to move things along at such times.

"She's on board," he said.

"Where is she sitting?"

"Far back, last row."

"Good. It fits," I said, tearing off the sheet and handing it out the window.

We started our left engine as we had the right. The propellers of the two engines unfeathered as I brought the condition levers forward, and they became invisible discs. The airplane shuddered with their increased speed and I felt it push against the brakes causing the nose to lurch a little forward. I waved off our North Platte marshaller, a young girl barely twenty-one, and she swung an orange wand toward the taxiway while trotting toward the warmth of the terminal.

The sun ignited the horizon as we rolled onto the asphalt taxiway by the end of the runway. My finger pressed the autofeather button, while Red mumbled his safety announcement into his microphone. I checked to see that he was actually broadcasting to the passengers instead of the outside world and found his switch in the proper position. A grasshopper clung to my windshield wiper; Red completed his announcement.

"Wasn't he here last week when we did this trip?" he asked.

"Apparently he wants to break his record."

"What was it last time?"

"As I recall, 90 knots."

"He's a regular daredevil, that one."

I pushed the power levers forward as we made the turn onto the runway, and then I pushed them up the rest of the way. The little 1900 accelerated nicely, pushing our backs into our seats. The grasshopper hung on.

"He's still there through seventy," Red said.

"Ninety."

"One hundred, he's still there, the bugger."

We rotated into the air. He disappeared.

"He made it to one hundred-ten. I think that's a record," he said.

"Gear up," I said.

Somewhere below, a few feet above the cornfields, there was a grasshopper flying through the air at breakneck speed. And somewhere not far away, there probably was a pretty girl grasshopper, maybe in an orange dress, swooning with delight at the show-off.

We drifted skyward with the rising sun warming the back of our fuselage as I reached behind me and closed the sliding pocket doors between the cockpit and the cabin, which gave us a little privacy. I bit into my éclair.

The broad section lines of the prairie below took on colors of emerald and auburn as the sun, through the curvature of the earth's atmosphere, created a colorful spectrum around us. I sipped coffee.

The twinkling dots of stars above faded into the nuance of a more pinkish ceiling gathering steam from below as we followed the twisting ribbon of the South Platte westward. The air was totally without nudging, though the concentric rings on the surface of my coffee vibrated to the hum of our engines. I believed I could safely finish it without any of it finding its way to my shirt. Red bit into his éclair and a bit of chocolate cream farted out the backside, but only just a little, and he licked it from his fingers with an 'ooh'. Another aircraft sped by in the opposite direction a few miles away giving us the impression that we were going very fast, yet the earth seemed to only meander by. We were obviously not alone for there were others sharing such pleasantries. Others, yes, because I saw in the glistening mirror of Lake McConaughy below, the telltale contrail of yet another airplane somewhere above us.

I thought, "This is the type of morning we aviators live for: silently sharing the experience of living in a work of art," as I finished my éclair.

Soon, Air Traffic Control switched us to a Denver Center controller who welcomed us with a, "Dandy Day," while the topmost spires of the Rocky Mountains glowed orange in the distance with the rising sun. The bottom half remained purple with the dwindling night. Denver came to life the nearer we came as the twinkling lights below faded like night stars on the ground; the roadways became darkened with commuters in cars on their way to work. I could see from the tip of Pike's Peak to beyond Long's Peak, a hundred miles and more.

Red dialed in the navigational frequencies for an approach as he did rain or shine, and we made a gradual bank toward Stapleton's 35 Left. We, humming in the sky like a giant bumble bee, twisted nearly perfectly over the city as Mount Evans made a grand view to our passengers, who I suspected might still be asleep in the tranquil contentedness of our blissfully uneventful flight...and missing the view. I lined up for the landing. The runway was much longer than our needs so I took my time. The little Beechcraft doesn't have the sizable struts that a larger jetliner has, and I used that as my excuse for not literally kissing the earth. But the landing was better than usual, mostly because there was nary a whisper of wind to spoil my flare, and of course, the runway seemed infinitely long.

"Nice one," Red lied.

I feathered the engine closest to the door, timing it so that the propeller would stop just as we pulled into our spot near the marshaller, and so that Red wouldn't have to crouch very long by the door. Our Denver marshaller gave me the "chocks in" sign as I killed the other engine. It didn't feel like an hour and twenty minutes had passed; the coffee, éclair and extraordinary view made the time go by quickly. Red turned the door handle and lowered the airstair carefully with the side cables, and jumped down the steps.

The passengers hurried down behind him with concerned looks on their faces. No one said, "Thank You," to Red; no one looked at him at all. They just kept their eyes forward, focusing on the entryway to the terminal as if they wanted to forget the last hour of their lives. One by one, they hurried off the airplane, quietly, except for one who said, "Thank God."

Lastly, the pretty woman in the orange dress came. Her face was gravely ashen. She walked slowly, maintaining distance from the others, moving the way an eighty-year-old woman moved. In comparing the mood of the sprightly beauty I saw board the airplane in North Platte to her present demeanor, I thought maybe I had really scared them. But how could I? It was a perfect morning.

She raised her head to speak though didn't look at me.

"I'm very sorry," she said. "I had a little accident."

I peered down the aisle and saw two vomit bags on the floor.

"Think nothing of it," I said. "That's why we have aircraft cleaners."

"Are you sure?" she said. "I feel so terrible about it."

"We'll take care of it. You have yourself a nice day," I said and smiled.

She hurried away toward the terminal leaving her eighty year old woman act behind.

"These North Platte people," I said as Red began straightening seatbelts and cleaning out seatback pockets, "are about the most polite people I have ever met."

"Yea—Uh, hold on there, chief," he said.

"Hmmm?"

He carefully bent over the filled vomit bags, which were not so neatly filled.

"That don't look polite at all."

"What's that you say?" I said.

"This ain't vomit and this ain't pee-pee," he said.

I froze with two seatbelts in my hands.

"Jesus."

"Look at it, it's everywhere."

"What the hell went on back here?"

"The seats, the armrests."

"The seatback pocket. Was it bumpy? I don't remember bumps."

"The floor, God, look at the floor."

"It must have been like sitting in an outhouse pit."

"The bags are full, two of them."

"Should have been more."

"Why didn't anyone say anything?"

"I don't know. Maybe they didn't want to bother us."

"But it's everywhere!"

Gasping for breathable air, Red said, "Want me to run inside and get her to clean this up?"

"No," I said. "You'll never see her face again."

The Entertainer

When you are an airline pilot, you are an entertainer except ideally you don't entertain with comedy, unless it is a comedy of errors. The entertainment for your audience is absolute. They give themselves up for the show, to experience all that our fingertips allow them. It is an intense drama sometimes, and when it is through, occasionally there is applause. However, applause is somewhat rare, because it implies that the outcome was in question. This was the night that, undeniably, the outcome was in question; my life, it seemed, was about to be extinguished.

The industry is filled with pilots who commute long distances to work. We do it because we can, but not always because we want to. We do it because Kansas City, and Atlanta, and sometimes New Guinea couldn't be our home. And, after uprooting our families once or twice or more times in the course of expansion and retraction of domiciles, we end up living in places far from our work. So, many of us commute until we learn that Kansas City, and Atlanta, and New Guinea aren't such bad places to live, given the alternative. The life of a commuting pilot then, not to be confused with a 'commuter pilot' who flies propeller driven planes for near poverty wages, is one generally dominated by thoughts of how to get to work and then home again. It becomes an obsession, checking the weather days in advance and trying to locate the cheapest hotel once he gets to his work city, trying to keep his expenses down—and hope that nothing cancels.

"Commuter pilots," on the other hand, are the ones who fly us commuting people around in propeller driven airplanes, beginning an hour before the crack of dawn and finishing their day three hours after sundown. They know they are paying their dues until the day they get the three-day-on four-day-off gigs. Most of us did it. Though I may sign in at work and fly one or two legs a day, down to Dallas and over to Tulsa, they fly eight short hops through the busiest sectors of air traffic control in the country: New York Approach. After they sign in, they skip on over to Buffalo, then LaGuardia, then Hartford, Boston, Martha's Vineyard, Albany, and right about the time their eyelids scrape on the pavement, they attempt the sleep of the dead in a two bit hotel with a drunk slamming doors down the hall all night. Then they get up before sun-up and do it all again.

The older I get, the younger the commuter pilots seem to get. I cannot forget, however, that by the time I was twenty-one, I was flying commuter planes for a living and I felt as comfortable doing that as I am nearly twenty years later. I try and remember that these guys and girls fly a thousand hours a year, and compared to a twenty thousand hour captain who may only fly a few hundred hours in a year in his final years before retirement, they have more recent, polished flying skills. They must demonstrate their proficiency in more stressful, closely watched, semi-annual proficiency checkrides, because the FAA and traveling public more closely scrutinize the younger lads. By the time we see them with their toe headed cowlicks and mildly scuffed flight bags getting on our planes, they have been wrung out sufficiently to fly me anywhere.

I ride as a passenger in the back of the bus with my suitcase on my lap along with everybody else. There are forty of us crammed in our seats and we are frustrated that the plane isn't ready as we sit in the bus on the tarmac in New York, twenty feet from the airstair door. Her wings rock gently under a raven, winter sky.

A black man in blue coveralls hops down the airstair and begins loading baggage into the front cargo compartment. A young, short-haired brunette appears at the top of the stairs and signals to our bus driver that it is okay to let us board. We are all quiet, seemingly ready to get this portion of our journey over with. No passenger is as in tune with the weather reports except me, since I just brought in a Boeing 737 from Saginaw. We stand and file like lemmings out of the bus and drop our carry-ons at the bottom of the aircraft steps. The black man picks them up two at a time and heaves them easily into the cargo compartment. The airplane seems small to me and well accustomed to hard work; its high wing is narrow and smudged with oil under her left engine; the paint has faded and is chipped. The forward side wall of the fuselage is dented where ice had been thrown off the propellers. I can see the captain's small hand protrude from a tiny door under his window as he hands a piece of paper to a ramp worker with yellow wands. It disappears back into the door. Though minuscule, that is all I see of him.

I take my seat by the window, mid cabin, on the right, close my eyes and listen again to the sounds of non-frequent flyers as they quip nervously about the smallness of the plane. At one time in history, a 50 passenger plane was a giant, but even I, perhaps because I checked the weather, or perhaps because I am just fatigued, feel it's too small tonight, too. The brunette, barely twenty-one, assumes her position in front of the microphone and begins her highly memorized safety speech, a speech that I have heard no less than a thousand times, yet can not remember a single line since I have so successfully learned to tune it out. I somehow end up with a row to myself and allow my knees to spread the width of the row.

Though young, the captain's voice is authoritative as he welcomes us over the address system. He tells the brunette to take her seat for takeoff. A multitude of strobes, flash in the sparkles of Kennedy Airport, as dozens of planes of every type wait to get out tonight. Small windows reveal dots of heads reading and sleeping and bickering and kissing in other airliners. Cockpits are black. We breeze by most of them and take the shorter runway, the one only commuter planes can use. Then the engines take on an aggressive sound as our propellers rip through the air. He releases the brakes and my ass finds every knot in the seat. We are airborne.

The cold front lies north of Albany and we aim toward it at almost three hundred miles an hour. She climbs out sluggishly, her body fat with New Yorkers, Vermonters, the occasional Montrealler, and eight college students coming home from break, and me, my eyes stinging from a very early show in Duluth and unable to read. So I can only stare out my window at the fading lights below, Manhattan long disappearing behind us as clouds creep ever thicker under and around us. The brunette, whose youthful face reveals pink pimples, works her way forward with the drink cart. I take a water. I feel a swath of wind against the tail, jarring us sideways momentarily and then we stabilize just as quickly. I gulp it and jam the cup into the seat pocket in front of me. The person in front of me cusses as he spills his coffee on his newspaper.

Tonight there is an ominous feeling in the air. Air is always changing, invisible yet alive, like an animal. Sometimes this animal is a sloth, moving at a snail's pace by the inch. Sometimes the air is like a tiger, randomly charging and whipping the neck of its prey. The pilot gets a sixth sense for the air. He can feel it in his thighs and fingertips as the control wheel fights gently at first, the urge to jostle the plane, and he distrusts what he feels. As the plane moves through the air, the wind barks at the side walls of the cockpit, taunting the crew, taunting most viciously because severe turbulence sometimes lurks in the blackness where one cannot see. Staring out at the blackness doesn't help find smoother air, yet it can be almost impossible to read the four inch wide attitude indicator, the only instrument capable of differentiating the sky from the ground, as your chin snaps against your sternum.

I know that our commuter pilot sitting in his seat tonight is paranoid. He read the reports of turbulence in the area, moderate in some places, and severe veiled in the reflected strobes deep within the wicked clouds. He looks out the window and picks up the microphone, presses the transmit switch, requests ride reports from other aircraft, asks for higher. He changes his seating position because he just noticed that his back hurts—psychosomatically. No one has gone through his area in a few hours. He would be the guinea pig, and the ripples aren't as they should feel as they cut at the aircraft menacingly.

There is a meanness in the air tonight. Not much is said between he and the first officer; there is an unspoken rule never to show fear, for to be afraid is to be in doubt, and doubt means mortality, something pilots must forget to stay sane. A joke will sometimes surface to release tension—nervous laughter. They think about anything but the inevitable, think of ways to avoid chaos. He flicks the seat belt sign on. The first officer clears his throat.

To say that the air is a tiger is not entirely correct. You can see a tiger and can anticipate its moves. A tiger can maul you with his large, white teeth should he capture you, but you at least have a fighting chance of getting away because you can see him. Wind can toy with you, play with you for hours, get ferocious and quickly subside, or just beat you mercilessly for hours, and you see nothing, cannot anticipate its next move because it is invisible. Fear is in the unseen. Fear lurks in the darkness. Fear is realizing that you happened to cross a monster of dismal proportions and are not sure when, or if, it will release you.

The ripples turn into waves crashing into the plane. Drinks spill, seat belts are tightened and bells ring in the cockpit; the flight attendant wants to know how long it's going to last. The captain apologizes to the cabin for the bumps, but is looking for smoother air. Air traffic control is no help; it's bumpy at all altitudes. Radar is useful, particularly at night...sometimes. Its primary function is to show areas of turbulence in the form of precipitation on a small screen in the cockpit in three distinct colors: green shows light precipitation; yellow shows moderate precipitation; and red, heavy precipitation. Before radar, flight crews had to avoid thunderstorms by steering away from lightning at night and staying in the clear or diverting to another airport, or, if need be, canceling the flight. But not all storms involve lightning, and by the time one sees lightning, it is often too late. Radar has made life easier in many ways for the pilot, but as with all technology, in as many ways that it has improved life, it has made it more complex. With radar, the pilot now has the ability to fly closer to thunderstorms than he may have otherwise, but radar is not infallible. Even when it is working right, sometimes there isn't enough precipitation in a storm to display echoes on the radar screen. If the pilot complacently relies on the radar as his only means of determining turbulence in the area, he inevitably gets caught off guard. And radar, for all its useful features, is of little use in the wintertime when there are no precipitation-fat thunderstorms, yet potentially more destructive winds.

Storms are as unique as individuals. Some storms may be so intense that to skirt through a "green" echo, which is normally associated with only light turbulence, may bring on such severe jolts that a flap track cracks or a gear door rips. The converse is also true, that some precipitation is so stable that even intense "red" echoes on the radar screen brings on only the lightest of ripples.

Green spots begin to filter in on the radar screen and frozen rain hisses against the windshield. Palms sweat. Nowhere on the radar is black, the color of nothing, no precipitation and maybe no turbulence. The captain banks the airplane gently to the right, but the view is the same. The ominous tiger is now patting the plane, nipping and boxing. The autopilot drops off line and consequently so does the flight director, the little needles on the attitude indicator that we get so used to following, and he grabs at the controls with both hands tightly, but thinks "loosely, loosely baby." The mind wants to grab, just as one wants to react more quickly when speed, in car or plane, increases. But the opposite is true. One must react more slowly as speed increases, or stress on the airframe increases with every jolt, and it is unnatural for the human body to react more gently as tension increases.

Flying a commuter airplane is in some ways more difficult than flying a heavy jet airliner. A commuter plane doesn't get much respect, because of its size, speed and the overall experience of her flight crew. Size rarely has anything to do with difficulty of flying, other than that potential collateral damage is greater in the event of a crash, but the flying is the same—take off, go to the destination, land. But propeller-driven commuter planes are more limited in performance, which makes them somewhat more challenging to fly than jet airliners. Because they are slower, commuter planes just fly at maximum speeds until the very last second in order to merge into the traffic pattern of a busy, jet intensive airport. But what mainly makes commuter planes more difficult to fly is their inability to get much higher than 20,000 feet. Below this, coincidentally, is the precise domain of the most intense storms. Often when a jet is flying in comfort at thirty-five thousand feet with its 'Fasten Seat Belt' sign off, and first class passengers are calmly being served smoked salmon, there is a commuter turboprop directly below at eighteen thousand feet in the midst of a temperature inversion and moderate turbulence, its passengers gripping armrests in fear. So the keenest sense for avoiding turbulence is developed quickly in the pilot's seat of a commuter airplane.

In the wintertime, the upper level jet stream winds dip low over mountainous terrain. As this wind touches the tips of the Adirondacks of northern New York, it begins a violent cycle of dips and rises and swirls, and rips its way over Lake Champlain and the Green Mountains of Vermont. By the time it gets to Mount Washington in New Hampshire, it roars across the peak at such a high velocity that a weather station there has recorded one of the highest wind speeds ever in the contiguous United States. Couple this with a common ice storm and therein brews a pilot's nightmare.

They say a pilot earns a year's worth of pay in ten minutes. The young captain has both hands on the controls of the turboprop and subsequently wipes the sweat from each palm on his knees quickly, never releasing a hand for more than a second from the wheel. A tingling sensation begins in his fingertips and gradually moves down his forearms as his increasing stress level constricts blood vessels to his extremities, and they begin to get uncomfortably cold and numb. A wave of wind crashes against his plane upending the left wing and he momentarily feels the stall warning stick shaker, warning him that there isn't enough airflow over the wing to maintain flight, and the automatic stick pusher jerks the nose down; two seconds later the overspeed clacker sounds saying he's too fast. He purposefully breathes to counteract subconscious hyperventilation. He pushes out air and inhales. How long has it been? How long since I took my last breath? he thinks. The first officer, who is normally very sharp, reaches for nothing, confused like a mouse caught in the three-walled end of a wrong turn in a maze. He has never experienced anything like this before; only one in a thousand pilots do.

The bottom falls out as though the plane had been sucked down a chute and the pilots are held only by their four point seat belts and then slammed onto their glutes back in their seats. Suitcases in the baggage compartment just behind the pilots tumble against restraining straps. A whiskey bottle breaks; the smell flares the nostrils of the captain, who is too concerned to equate it with anything out of the ordinary.

Nothing is said between the pilots; nothing can be done but to hold on. The copilot groans at the next jolt and the bottom falls out again. He bites his tongue as his jaw slams shut. The captain slaps his hand on his thigh to get blood flowing back into it. Five hundred feet is lost in the blink of an eye and, as soon as it is regained, it is lost again with an additional five hundred. The air traffic controller is concerned about the altitude loss and has cleared them with a two thousand foot block altitude. The captain wonders if he can maintain the aircraft within that block.

Severe turbulence is rare. It is more commonly reported by very small aircraft, because they tend to get tossed around so much more intensely. These turbulence reports are usually from a voice on the radio trembling in fear. Though airplanes rarely burst apart in severe turbulence, it is generally the opinion of most pilots, that the sole reason their airplanes stay aloft is the pilot's skill and ability to maintain the appearance of calm in the heart of the tempest. They fight, but they don't fight, they pray, but know no god, they wish for help, but automation is useless, and an air traffic controller has all but any control. And the other pilot, the first officer, is there entirely for moral support—a breathing, warm body that is sharing the predicament and immeasurably useful for that alone.

As we burst into the front, the seat belt sign illuminates immediately; the captain asks all to remain seated with a boyish crack. The games begin.

There is an unevenness in the drone of the propellers, only blackness in the clouds outside my window. It is as though we are an audience watching our own lives participate in this drama, wondering what will happen next. The ice inspection lights flash on and I can see we are accumulating a moderate amount of ice on the black boots on the leading edge of the wing. The clouds reflected in the lights flash by in poofs revealing our speed and then the blackness returns as the light is switched off. The lady in seat 2D grabs her armrest, startled by the sound of ice popping against the fuselage at near supersonic speed four inches from her head. The propeller heat is working. Again, a blast of ice smashes against the fuselage; heads turn. I watch.

The turbulence increases, and though I, too, am a pilot, it is different in the back of the plane. I do not know our exact attitude, I do not grip the bird in my cold hands, I do not share the responsibility of lives when I am strapped payload in the back. I am a lemming, a rat behind the pied piper. But with each jolt, my solar plexus stiffens and I am nauseated with increasing butterflies. I know by approximation what our position is and it occurs to me that deadly severe turbulence lurks somewhere in this dreary night. My own impatience with my commute had not allowed me to swallow my pride and spend the night at an overpriced hotel in New York. And it is at this moment that I would have traded positions with any cubicle-shackled individual.

As we cross over the ridges of the Green Mountains, the wind roars across us with a ferocity I have never imagined. Three hundred knots is merely a number on a gauge until it is hit in the face with an opposing hundred and fifty-knot wall of angry wind. I've seen steel girders bend in post hurricane footage, hurricane winds that never come close to the combined oncoming torrent that we are now passing through, and all the while, as I strain to keep an eye out the window I see our white wing above flexing, twisting, bending, flapping, but not disappearing, not releasing us under the strain. I am amazed at the engineer.

Have you ever…
Sparred with the devil
On a moonless night,
When you found yourself alone;
Surrounded by ten thousand strobes,
Living in the foam?

Have you been...
Whisked away
To the forlorn edge;
In a timeless nightmare;
Of granite clouds and burnt thunder,
Pounding like a sledge?

Now you have!

Screams infest the cabin, and like dominos, more screamers scream. We are thrashed, flogged, lashed, beaten, pummeled. It occurs to me that in the chaotic blackness of the night, the pilots can no better see the few instruments required to know where the horizon is than I can see the bald headed cusser in front of me.

There is nothing more heinous than to be the mouse in the mouth of a thrashing cat, to have no control as you watch and feel your life slip away. Again the monster wave crashes against our craft and the plane rolls violently. I hear a groan in unison as every soul is hit with the same thought. My first thought as I open my eyes is, "At what point did I close my eyes?" and, "How long were they closed?" and, "Was that me groaning, too?" It was the, "It is inevitable; I will die tonight with these people" groan, and I heard it faintly from my own lips. Surely it would be an impossibility for us to land safely in this, I think. How they fought valiantly up front to save this ship, I could only imagine as I tightened my own belt again. How bravely they stuck to their controls, fighting the insurmountable beast just trying to get my ass to Vermont! They are mortally limited humans like me, and I am not tricked into believing they are as all knowing and powerful as the non-flyer has been led to believe.

And then the punishment stops, and the wings right, and the droning becomes even, and my heart races on. I release my fingers from my own arm rests but sit, paranoid, thinking the next will surely snap the wings off—me, the silly fool in the pilot suit, still anticipating, my jaded mistrust for nature getting the better of me.

But as she drones on, writhing in mere moderate whips while farmhouse lights below fade in; we approach our destination. My breath steams the window as I see the ground in a normal-looking descent. No one chatters, no one reads, no one turns his head, but looks straight on, for I wasn't the only one who believed we were doomed, and it is odd to force myself to now believe that indeed a longer life on this earth is possible—nay, probable.

The lights grow in intensity and numbers as we near. I can make out the shapes of small homes and buildings as our turbo-propeller airplane flies over them. We jump at the sound of the thump of the main gear releasing and I can hear the wind as it presses on the open gear doors. My rattled nerves embarrass me. I note how small the engines look, and how the twigged branches of winter maples below spread like rows of spiders along Williston road. Two headlight beams from a lone car wander along the road, maybe toward a comrade of mine, maybe the cusser's wife. The captain tells the brunette to be seated in a very short, very racked tone, and I watch in disbelief as the ground so nonchalantly nears our tires.

It is not a spectacular landing in any normal sense. It isn't smooth, or straight. In fact, it is as if the man in the left seat gave up trying six inches above the concrete knowing that to get us this far was miraculous. We touch down once or twice, and the little engines that powered through that insanity, so cherished, roar into reverse, and he over brakes sloppily. Given the circumstances, the mere fact that he had strength enough in his shaky knees to apply brakes is a wonder.

The left engine whines down and the propeller feathers. I can see the ground marshaller wave us in. We stop and the other engine feathers, the electric hydraulic pump whines as it normally does. The door opens. I sit composing myself, dispelling my own shaky knees. The cusser stands and pulls on an overcoat over his shoulders, and for the first time realizes that he sat in front of a pilot. He looks at me angrily, as though I should have warned the crew not to scare him so badly.

"What the hell happened?" he says.

I look at the man for the longest moment, trying to think of a scientific explanation as to why his body isn't in little pieces in a hole fifty miles south of our position. My lips move to explain the winter wave effect—the lowering of the jet stream that crashes against mountainous impediments, but stop instead, and without prior thought, I begin to clap, clapping hard, hoping that the pilots ahead of the locked door can hear. Another joins in, then others. We are alive. We have experienced the ride of our lives, having resigned ourselves to be at the mercy of nature and yet were where we wanted to be—home—because of the will that our pilots had to live, because they never gave up as they could have, and others had before.

The cusser just puts on his hat, grunts, and slips on the ice on his way to the terminal.

On the Ground a Pilot is Just Another Fish Out of Water

Midnight, and I drag deeply on the Canadian cigarette. Above, the stars glisten, and street traffic diminishes as two musicians sit on the curb by my feet conversing in French. Their black tuxedos smell of smoke and perspiration, their ties dangle untied. The bassist flicks his cigarette in the parking lot and coughs, and the drummer looks on as the butt sparkles with orange embers as it tumbles. I drop mine and snuff it inconspicuously under my heel, blow skyward. The smoke disappears from my nostrils. I sense the sweetness of May in the air and my vision clears, though I'm tangibly inebriated.

Just beyond the door, in the great hall, a recording of old dance tunes infiltrates the reception as the band takes a break. The excitement of the party faded the moment they unplugged their instruments and walked out. They don't seem so glamorous sitting on the curb by my feet as they did moments earlier when I stared in amazement at their talent. They are just men with scuffed shoes and cheap wristwatches, talking. A few minutes earlier the girl with the microphone belted, "I Want A Man To Rock Me," seemingly at me, no one else, causing me great yearning for her at the time. Her eyes twinkled in the stage lights, her cherry-red lower lip quivered in my direction. I was in love. Now, at a small table beside the stage, a piece of cheese sticks to her chin as she stuffs her cherry smudged lips with wedding lasagna in a way that is distinctly anticlimactic.

People file in and out through the double glass doors. There is laughter beyond the restrooms. Men and women walk arm in arm. The bride scurries by, then disappears back into the reception, her angelic white dress draws my eyes. I light another, flick twice, inhale, exhale.

I stand leaning against the stucco wall of the building, fixated on the strobe of an object drifting six miles above, a rumble barely audible; thinking.

Two days earlier I stood in front of the right engine of my 737. I reached in and grabbed a fan blade and spun the engine checking for worn bearings. It clicked as it turned, as it should, and I knelt below in search of the telltale oil puddle that eluded me again. The nacelle is a beautiful example of sculpted engineering artistry hung below the Boeing's swept wing. In a passing glance, I caught the eye of a young boy in a horizontal red striped shirt as he waved from the terminal window. Perhaps he thought it was against the rules, by the look of surprise on his face as I stood and waved back, and he jumped. Six others in the window smiled. They were either going with me or seeing off a loved one; either way, I was their entertainment. I tucked in my shirt and continued with the preflight, thinking, *This is where I belong.*

The wheel-well is slick with a mucky mixture of oil, hydraulic fluid, and charred tire smoke. The sun warms the pavement as it beams between the clouds in heavenly fingers in the New York sky. It had rained within the hour. The smell of ever-present kerosene drifts about me in a ghostly meandering; men on the ramp near me heave luggage on the belt loader and stack them in the belly; another connects the pushback tug with loud thunks and clangs. The fueler hands me a pink fuel slip. I thank him. He grins Indian corn teeth, and I have to chuckle.

I walk aboard through the Jet Bridge and a stunning blonde greets me wearing black stilettos, as she kneels in the galley. Her form is that of a cover girl, with nary a fold to the skirt she wears so perfectly about her hourglass waist, and she winks as though I was an old friend. She stands and I catch myself staring, but only momentarily, as she thrusts her hand in my direction and introduces herself.

"Christine," she says. My fingers envelop hers, and they clench. She motions toward another equally enchanting girl to come meet me. She is our lead, Traci with an "i." I also see the form of another beauty, checking her compartment for the usual safety devices. They all move about like dancing fairies. Working with such beautiful women is one of the most cherished, yet unspoken, perks of being an airline pilot.

I move to the right half of the cockpit, the place where I sometimes feel more at peace than in my own bed at home. I drop my brain bag to the right of my seat, pull the latch, and slide my lower half onto the worn sheepskin. Out of habit, I grip the control wheel, the horns of the sleeping bull, and gently pull. She's a tough old bird with a ten thousand hour mush. I lean back in my seat and regard the array of switches, and consider the implausibility of them all. Then I close my eyes and listen to the sounds of the unflighted cockpit: gyros whir; the standby altimeter vibrator tics; the ramp controller chatters on the captain's side speaker in typical frenzy. I hear a tiny giggle from the back, and a baggage compartment door gently thumps as it is closed.

Then, like a steam locomotive, I chug alive as I move about unpacking my brain bag, toss open my Jepps and plug in my headset. Switches fly, and I scratch down weather; I adjust pedals; I set settings in instruments, and I make hand signals to the ground people to pull our umbilical. I set the brakes, and bang the APU relays.

The captain comes aboard. He appears to be John Wayne's twin as he slaps my back and jams his hat on a clip on the wall. I tell him he could have spent another minute or two flattering Traci with an "i."

After a New York rain shower, the air is without dust. The cityscape glistens in the evening sun, nestled beneath the diving shadows of arrivals abeam the runway. Every minute an airplane lands and another departs, yet there is a constant hundred giant birds squatting below the control tower like chicks in a brooder. We are just another number in this endless crowd, sharing the glory of living in a time when so much excitement rests in the giddy knuckles of a chosen few.

To the uninitiated, the beast of New York can be daunting. The controllers are unforgiving, spitting acid at those who daydream while their taxi clearance goes unacknowledged. Working efficiently within this environment, following the conga line to the runway end and departing this perpetual puzzle, embodies the maximum complexity of all that this profession allows, and I am at my apex here, dealing with whatever they throw at us. Stern looks are few anymore from the man on the left, as over the years I have managed to allow the tiny drips of knowledge to seep into the granite rock that is my brain, not unlike Chinese water torture, and I relax.

To be one with the sky, flying wistfully beyond the limits of the land-locked's greatest dream, is the realization that there is a paradise some-where. I have seen it, I have been there, I am there frequently in fact; it is in part over New York City. We level where angels lurk. Behind every crevasse, every puff of graduated white that transcends transonically, they watch enviously as our Boeing thunders by.

I have learned to forget what I do, as all pilots do. I have learned that by repeatedly pointing airplanes skyward, starting with small ones as a teen-ager and gradually increasing them in size to what I only hope is eventually a 747, I can trick myself into thinking that there aren't a hundred and fifty loved humans trusting their lives to my judgment. Moreover, as I take them at speeds over five hundred miles an hour and contemplate a landing in a gusty blizzard, I trust that all the knowledge I have gained doesn't drain out of my head somehow down the line. My greatest nightmare is waking up from this dream life, seated alone at the controls without a clue what I'm doing. And because of this, while I sleep in my bed at home, I occasionally bolt upright drenched with sweat.

Two knocks and the cockpit door opens. I see steaks on trays, hot tow-els, magnetized silverware, a chunk of sweet San Franciscan chocolate, brought to me by Traci with an "i." The aroma of seared beef permeates the cockpit mixing with the permanent oleo-electric-bodily fragrance of an airplane. I know this is too good to be true.

I can remember the first hot meal I received as an airline pilot; it was Chicken Cordon-Bleu and green beans. I stared in amazement at it for a very long time while sitting at my Second Officer's panel back then, before I understood that it was mine. So I cut it into the tiniest of fractions of suc-culent chicken breast and nibbled miserly on each delicious piece; it was a feast as good as any Thanksgiving. It was at that moment that I felt I had achieved what I had yearned for after years of eating cold peanut butter and jelly sandwiches while flying with propellers—a hot crew meal, not overcooked, not undercooked, done just right, just for me and brought right to me, no less. It was at that moment that I understood what it meant to be a pilot for a major airline.

I eat vigorously.

I am home in my seat. That's not to say that there are no problems, or that I am without worry. It is where I am most comfortable—as much as one can be comfortable, while also sitting on the edge of potential catastrophe. These men and women who sit to my left are my family; I accept them for what they are, which can be peculiar given the profession. Life has a different meaning for a pilot than it does for the rest of the world. That one can sit day after day, geared to react to a multitude of explosions of any sort, can change how we approach life. I have seen jumpy men whose eyes dart at the faintest, unusual sound. I have seen the opposite, those who, with smoke pouring from unknown locations, wish to continue with the three-hour flight, firmly seated in denial. I have seen the truest heroes who regard any emergency with such a calmness that I cannot describe, not men or women who spit orders from sub paragraphs in manuals, but those who have an air of confidence…assuredness in every situation, speaking from the heart. I believe any problem can be solved with them. Call it charisma.

These people are my brothers and sisters, my fathers and mothers, my sons and daughters. They sit beside me, opening themselves up in ways that only intimate family members can. I learn of divorce proceedings, infidelity, terminal illnesses, great pain and great longing, all in the course of my first two hours with a recent stranger. We share thoughts so deep that to leave the cockpit would constitute monumental betrayal, as there is an unspoken swearing of secrecy once wings are pinned. I am their therapist as they are mine. They are my home.

We encounter the runway in Cancun in the way penguins transition from sea to glacier. The runway is patched with uneven asphalt and we can only guess where the center is by the lack of a painted centerline for almost half of it. As we touch, we rumble over patches until the steady jiggling of our upper torsos, like a washboard, causes uncontrollable laughter. It is a long runway and the farther down we go the more our bodies shake. We park. The main door is opened and I inhale eastern Mexico's fragrant humidity.

For a pilot, home is not a building with four walls and a roof, neither is it wherever his hat is laid; it is that area in closest proximity to his plane. It is the only area in which he knows unconditional love, where rules are plainly understood, and all who gather there are accepted. It is the only place where an aviator knows for sure he belongs, the only place he knows what day it is—exact Zulu time for that matter. Home is Chicago, San Juan, Tokyo, and Berlin, all at once, so long as jets rumble his hotel room window there. Home is walking the beach in Tampa with shiny black Florsheims, sandals in Milwaukee in January, paying twelve dollars (US) for a hamburger at the hotel restaurant, and administering parental advice over the telephone from a thousand miles away. Home is sharing dinner at a Japanese restaurant in Mexico with four people you met four hours before. Home is the Ramada in Buffalo on Christmas morning.

The twinkling strobe disappears among a sea of stars over Quebec. The Big Dipper is slashed by its fading contrail, barely visible by the moon's ghostly light. This is the same set of stars that hovers over me wherever I stray in the northern hemisphere, following me the way a collection agency follows a debtor. I suck in burned cigarette filter and wince at the bitter smoke. I spit and flick the smoldering butt, crumple what's left of my pack, jam it into a can by the doors, and reenter the building.

The band members returned some time ago to their home: the stage. I hear guitars twang as they tune up again. The pretty girl with the cherry-red lips once again could melt the heart of any man. She smiles at someone else this time and I am jealous. In her element, she is magnificent.

French is spoken everywhere and, but for the graceful sound of it, I am unaware of what is said. People wander about the dimly lit dance floor, beautiful people in colorful gowns and black tuxedos with ascots and cummerbunds, hair glazed—both men and women. They laugh, they eat from an endless supply of hors d'oeuvres, they mingle. I recognize a few and we stumble through conversations in broken French and broken English. The band strikes a beat, and the party once again takes off with intensity.

In the darkness of the room, surrounded by such splendor, I am alone. I am a spectator, a fish flopping on dry land. These people will sleep in their own beds tonight. Monday, they will most likely work, in my opinion, someplace benign. They will eat at their usual time, sleep at their usual time, and not feel like it's 10:00 when it's only 3:00. They will see faces of neighbors they have seen for years. They will, in fact, be synchronized.

I watch the band play and long for home, I long to be thirty-three thousand feet above the world.

Tuesday with Catillano

His hotel room echoes with rowdy laughter just north of the airport. Captain Catillano fills his plastic cup, floating the tiny pips of ice that once diluted the vodka, and fills each of our own cups in turn. No one was asked; it was just assumed that the beverage should be drained out of his sterling flask, and no one refused. He shakes the last few drops out of it into my cup and apologizes for not filling it to the top, then lights a cigar—so does Taylor, by pressing the end of her brown stogie onto his lit cherry and sucking like a mackerel. Soon his non-smoking room fills with the guano-scented smell of contraband Cubans, but no one cares. The television plays "The Sopranos" in the background. Taylor appears with a towel from the bathroom.

The nor'easter sprays pellets of snow like a natural sandblaster against the window. Wind whistles through the cracks in the aluminum window frame, and the cracks around the wall air conditioning unit, which also rattles as it produces heated air. Outside, past my open drape, fluorescent lights in the parking lot teeter above swirling moths of snow making eerie shadows in mounds that once were cars. There is only blackness in the night just beyond those lights, blackness where I know snow spreads out like a blanket of cotton in the field beyond the razor-wire fence, toward the prison lights.

Cheap perfumes freshen my nostrils against the smoke.

"Now, how does this go?" Tina asks, looking in Taylor's direction.

"This towel goes around the top part of your head, covering your eyes," she says.

"And you have to guess what I want you to remove, and keep removing items until you remove the piece that I was thinking of," Catillano lisps through his cigar, and winks at me as though we are fraternal brothers. "It's

- 58 -

the only true initiation into the airline business. We all went through it, eh kids?"

"Sure, yeah," we say.

"Oh, okay then," she says.

This is the first day we flew together as a crew. Catillano had been around since long before deregulation, the days when a crew was not a crew but a family, albeit a family of alcoholics sometimes. You can see by the stiffness in his shoulders, his coiffed gray hair, and the way he wears his abused hat on a forty-five degree angle, that he had spent many years sitting at hotel bars killing time and honing his image.

"You must be thinking of my shoes. I'm giving you my shoes," she says, and kicks them off.

"Nope, not your shoes," he replies.

"Then," she says leaning back, "I guess I have to remove this." She unbuttons her shirt more slowly than I had hoped, revealing her full brassiere, and then she throws the shirt in his direction.

My breathing shortens momentarily, Taylor chuckles, and Nancy says, "Good Lord."

"Nope, that is not what I'm thinking of either. Nice try."

There are men who fly as though it was a job. They sign for the airplane and speak of important things like weather and fuel loads. They call their wives between stops to say they are okay; they talk of children's soccer matches on long hauls between cities regardless of whether anyone wants to hear about them or not. They are real family men, their shirts are neatly pressed by caring wives, and shoes scuff-less. When they finish for the day, they kick the dust of the job from their heels and hope to forget about it the minute they block in. There are also men who say that to fly for a living is to find a way to get from party to party. They have few worries except for who will *slam-click* them that night and who will be playing. They surround themselves with booze, and those who make booze their religion, and if they are lucky enough to be a captain, they can surround themselves by polite listeners of ragged, old stories that even *they* have lost interest in. They had wives and mortgages and sometimes a boat once, but those are long gone along with most of the money they had saved. So their home *is* work. Ideally, and it is rare, they find themselves among a crew of similars, people who fly for the same reasons, to get away from their troubles, as if the jet plane itself was a bottle of Scotch.

That afternoon we aimed toward the great northeast, approaching a cold front over Pennsylvania. Our Boeing 737's anti-ice, both engine and wing, melts ice before it can load us down, and ice pellets hiss on the windscreen. There is nothing but the whiteness of winter before us, but the radar shows green in various thicknesses ahead. Snow, sleet, rain and hail live within the green. Airplanes are stuck in holding patterns a hundred miles northeast of our position. Catillano, anticipating this, eases the throttles almost to idle as we slow to two-thirty.

His seatbelt strap dangles unnoticed into the mug of hot water by his right knee. The water turns a murky gray-brown immediately. I see the strap soaking in his mug.

"Tea of a thousand Asses," I say, and reply to an order to hold our present heading with air traffic control.

"Tea of a thousand Asses? Are you implying something about my character, or of fellow captains?" he says, and I laugh.

"Just a dirty belt."

As we burn our precious fuel, being sent off course away from our destination, I tap the computer for a new weather message. A few minutes later it chimes and the printer spits.

"Get a load of this," I say, as I pull the weather.

Behind the cockpit door, working the first class cabin, Nancy brings a second pillow to a blue haired woman with tuna fish breath. The rabbit of a man beside her pretends to hear his wife's complaining as he retreats toward the window. He secretly wishes for a heart attack, hers, or if need be, *his*. Nancy offers her a blanket, but is met with only a fishy scowl. The airplane jolts again as we encounter the cold front and a man two rows up chimes her to take what is left of his cup of coffee. She takes it while traversing the bumps with the grace of a woman who has done it ten thousand times before. Her own years of sincere smiling had departed with her third husband and she has succumbed to being a flight attendant until she dies. She pulls out the P.A. microphone and makes an announcement for everyone to remain seated since the fasten seatbelt sign is on. She smiles; then she glances at a tiny mirror on the wall next to the galley oven and looks away, hating the way her cheeks have become lined like a New York City road map.

"A big nor'easter is hitting the east coast," I say.

"Nor'easter," he says. "How I miss the days when all we had to worry about were mere blizzards."

I scan the printed weather and hand it over to him.

"Low pressure sitting out over the Atlantic, a constant fifty mile an hour wind with horizontal snow, that's what it is."

He looks at the fuel gauges.

"It'll be tight."

Tina and Taylor in the far back roll the bar cart toward the aft galley preparing to secure it, and they grab unconfidently at the overhead bins for balance. Taylor's thigh rubs hard against a suited salesman's forearm. He inhales her perfume and contentedly eases back into his seat as the child seated next to him cries.

Taylor's stomach is empty, as it usually is. She thought that to be slender and firm with an attractive face and long hair was enough to find happiness and a decent man, but the men she meets are, to her, shallow, or mean, or worthless. At twenty-nine she is at the height of her beauty and she knows it. But she is willing to continue patiently trying to find herself a sincere man, one who loves her for being her, as she seriously contemplates a boob job.

Tina is the youngest flight attendant at twenty-one. She lives with her parents, but considers herself a worldly adult, though she still hides her cigarettes from them, and gives her little brother an occasional pack for not telling. She often thinks about checking her cell phone, though the messages are usually from her mother. She lives for adventure, so long as it isn't too far from home.

"How much longer on this heading?" I ask over the radio.

"Another fifty miles, then I'll turn you in," he replies.

We are going into the thick of the squall and the airplane is lurching as we begin holding over Pennsylvania. I hear over the company operations frequency that one of our Caribbean arrivals is diverting to Baltimore.

"We got about ten minutes of this before bingo."

"Gotcha," he says.

The cockpit interphone chimes.

"How long is this going to last?" asks Nancy.

"Till we get there, dear," he says.

A young boy throws up in the back and his mother lashes at him verbally.

"Looks like we have a puker back here."

"You have to go?"

"The girls are handling it. Do you need anything up there?"

"Two chubbies and a malt."

"Just ran out."

In back, Taylor rubs bits of the child's vomit from the salesman's trousers; he closes his eyes and wishes for it never to end.

As we near our bingo, the amount of fuel we cannot go below lest we not make our alternate, the Center controller begins clearing aircraft in.

"Delta Two-Fifty-Six cleared via present position direct to Sweet intersection."

"Delta Two-Fifty-Six direct Sweet," they reply.

"United Twelve-Ninety-Three, New York Center..."

"I hate this," I say, "there's bingo."

"He should clear us any second," says Catillano. "How's the weather in Philly?"

"About the same."

As I keyed the mike to request a reroute to our alternate, we are cleared to resume the arrival.

"Good tailwind," he says.

In the cabin, less shimmering light flashes through a hundred oval windows as we pass through thickening clouds. Darkness eventually prevails and tiny reading lights make up for most of the existing illumination, though reading is nearly impossible in the lurching and jarring airplane. Most of the people are forced to either look out the window, or ahead of them at their neighbor's wrinkled bald spot, which doesn't help their nausea. Nothing does. Not the cooler air that I tune into the ducts, not the slower airspeed—nothing.

Tina wishes she was home baking cookies with her mother.

"Tell me about Charles," she asks Taylor, mostly wanting to get her mind off of her queasiness.

Taylor, sitting in the jumpseat across from Tina, looks up from her dull-eyed stare at the floor.

"He was a wimp," she says barely audibly.

"Sorry about that."

"He's gone now, thankfully. He found himself some little college girl to impress," she mumbles, trying not to jostle her head.

Tina knew her man would be different, whoever he was. Taylor suddenly gagged, unbuckled, and ran into the lavatory and shut the door.

Below, and two hundred miles ahead and beyond the sight of New York Harbor, thirteen ships thrash in the churning sea. Waves reach over eighteen feet as frozen water charges over bows. Men in rain gear grab onto rails to keep from sliding overboard and ship captains scream orders to turn into the swells. But no matter how rough the ocean is, no matter how relentless the charging water is, it is not the adversary that invisible, powerful, and vicious air is.

"Roger, right heading one-twenty," I say on the radio.

"How much longer are they going to vector us around like this?" I complain. I can feel our luck spiraling down. My stomach tingles with butterflies.

"Whoa there, girl, where are you goin'?" Catillano says to the airplane as he manhandles it to the new heading. She tries to shake him, but he won't let her. He's a cowboy breaking in a bronco, in his mind.

"Sir, there's going to be just one shot at the airport. We are sitting on a little more than an hour's worth of fuel at this very moment. Philly isn't a good option."

He smiles crooked, tea-stained teeth, "A nor'easter's like pretty woman—always tempting you to go places you have no business being. We'll make it," he says. "We have to anyway, regardless of where we go. Philly, Baltimore, Boston, it's all going to be down to the nuts."

He intercepts the glide slope and we are thrown into our belts with a sideways crack of wind.

"I think I'll need a little solace once we get on the ground," I say.

"You know where you find that, don't you?" Catillano says without taking his eyes from the instruments.

"Yeah, the bar."

"No," he says, "it's in the dictionary, right between gonorrhea and syphilis. Now, throw the gear down."

Tina bolts for the other lavatory and heaves her partly digested chicken sandwich into the stainless steel toilet bowl. She continues dry heaving uncontrollably, as does Taylor in the opposing lavatory. Overhead call buttons chime, but Nancy can't move to aid the passengers in their bouts with airsickness. She wonders where the other two are, but doesn't wonder for long when she notices the swishing back end of the plane, like a ride on the "Tilt-A-Whirl."

Catillano begins a tirade of obscenities as if it would make flying the approach any easier.

"Ruffer'n a c-cob," I manage.

"Flaps fifteen, and gimme a landing checklist," he commands through the buffeting. "Airspeed is all over the place!"

I hate this. I hate that we are shy on fuel. I hate that we didn't divert the first moment the thought crossed my mind. I hate that I didn't stand more firmly when that thought hit me. I hate that I wasn't sure at all. But I wouldn't want to be him. Sure, my butt is on the line just as much as Catillano's, but he's the one with the bull's horns in his hands. He's the one, who in the back of my mind, after the fire subsides and our smoking carcasses are shoveled up in a backhoe, I can say "told you so, you dope." I wouldn't want to be him. I hate this.

"Flaps thirty, keep an eye out."

"The guy two planes ahead is going around," I say.

"Don't you think I know that?"

"You're coming up on minimums."

He lets out what normally ends up as the last thing heard on a cockpit voice recorder—a loud, long sequence of profanities that no sane man could conjure.

"I see it, approach lights ten o'clock!" I scream.

He aims for the smear of bobbling lights. If he didn't, our chances of making a better approach to another runway would be just as bad. The one light leads to another one and then a larger group of bobbling lights, jumping in a sea of snow-white. The wind has us cocked like a weathervane and he kicks the pedals to slip us into alignment with the runway. The nose sways in the gusts and he jacks the throttles to keep the 737 under control.

The profanities continue.

Bang! Goes the right main. Bang! Goes the left. Throttles snap to full reverse; snow flies all about. The nose rattles on the icy pavement as if driven on washboards. He stomps on the brakes and I am thrust into my shoulder harness.

We slow to taxi speed and ease off the runway, and he sets the brakes. Silence.

It is as though we woke from a dream and all is right again. New York is its normal, befuddled self—chatter here, chatter there.

He is winded, as though he just ran wind sprints for the last half hour. My heart must be beating as fast as his I suppose, and though our cockpit is cold, I notice my forehead, arms and back are moist.

Silence.

Taylor leaves the lavatory just before Tina does, their nausea departing once they feel solid ground under the floor, and they take their respective jumpseats in the back. Tina is convinced that she will never fly again. When she gets to the hotel, she plans on calling her father immediately and telling him that she will go back to school and finish her degree as long as she never has to set foot in another airplane. Taylor is resolved to grab the first man who shows her the slightest bit of attention, regardless of how he acts, so that she can quit and let him support her for awhile. Life is too short to have to put up with such anxiety, such illness. No man can be as bad as that last approach, she thinks. Nancy just sits in the front jumpseat facing the wall in front of her. She doesn't think of quitting, because she can't. She doesn't think of a man saving her, either, for the same reason. She is just resolved to come back and do it again if need be, and is beyond caring.

The cabin interphone chimes and Nancy picks up.

"Drinks on me," Catillano says.

She cracks a furtive smile.

The car horns of tense New York attitude contrast our weary crew as we wait in the usual spot by the curb for the hotel van. We are mostly quiet in the wind and snow, in our own worlds, and deflated, except for Catillano who can sense the oncoming euphoria, the reason he so many times finds himself in the bar and other places with his crew.

Some may think that sharing a grueling experience might necessitate separation after it is over, but it fuses people together in a way that only airline flying can. Our hearts were in our throats, and thoughts of mortality entered more than once in the last hour, something no other job evokes. But when it is all over, with firm earth solidly beneath our feet, the feeling of relief is overwhelming. It is like a mother in childbirth, pushing through the pain, wondering not only if she will survive, but if her child will be healthy, or even alive itself. But then the baby comes, the pain is over, and the blood ceases to drain from her, and memories of the ordeal disappear.

She becomes intoxicated with the joy of a successful birth, and a burst of natural dopamine. She may even contemplate another one someday.

The brain is a curious thing. Scientists have only touched the surface of the inner workings of the human brain and what motivates us to do certain things, and survive stresses, and how to avoid becoming generally psychotic. The body produces its own form of physical pain relief in response to painful stimuli, both physical and mental, which is as potent as a high dose of morphine. Psychologically, when we face the stress of landing our plane in this nor'easter, low on fuel, and eventually survive it, our brains release the neurotransmitter dopamine, which is not unlike a high dose of cocaine or alcohol, and we are all giddy an hour after the ordeal is over.

Catillano knows this.

We look at each other in a familiar way now, this crew who a day before were all strangers. None of us is above or below the other, we are all the same, having shared something that no one else, even intimate family members, have shared. Slam clicking would be unimaginable tonight. The Hotel van arrives, stopping a few feet from our feet, and the driver hops out to load our bags. Catillano gingerly assists the girls up the step by holding their elbows as though they were precious cargo, and I recall a joke that elicits hoots.

Back in the hotel room, Tina unbuttons her skirt. We look at each other in amazement. How long shall we let this go on?

Inebriated, Tina begins pulling her skirt below her thighs. Nancy shakes her head in disbelief.

"Tina, honey, that is not what I am thinking of either," he says.

"Oh, I know what you are thinking of there, mister," she says, and reaches around her back to undo her bra. Carefully and deliberately her thumb slides underneath the little metal clasp as she flicks at the fabric with her index finger. Her full bosoms strain against the cups as she lies there on the bed, causing the clasp to knot the fabric. She grunts with her arms behind her, leaning forward, twisting at the stubborn connection. Catillano and I can't believe our good fortune. Soon the room will be filled with the voluptuous presence of her womanly appurtenances.

"No! Tina, before you go on…" Catillano interjects, "I am thinking of the towel. That is the only thing I wanted you to remove."

She stops, after her fingers partly disconnect the clasp, realizing that she just removed much more than she needed, and throws the towel at him.

They are like Bullets

They are like bullets that move very fast, are unseen, and potent. In this rare moment, they are captured together, frozen in space and time around a table in a room underneath the busy concourse. They sit while the snow accumulates outside. They sit while the departing and arriving airplanes slow to a trickle, then stop altogether. They sit though it is alien for them to remain in one place for long. But there they stay, for once not in command of their own lives, for they have finally met an adversary more powerful than themselves. Though they live in motion at velocities close to the speed of a bullet in flight, there they sit—frozen quicksilver.

Outside, the wind howls against the windows, against the terminal, and against the trucks with the flashing yellow lights. They are losing the battle against the blizzard as the truck augers spit geysers of white powder against it. The sky is determined to have its way. Bulging with snow and ready to burst at any moment, it teases unrelentingly, and overwhelmingly spreads drifting mounds of snow wherever it pleases. To fight the onrush of winter is futile tonight and every worker in every truck knows it, yet they continue to remove what a minute later is replaced, mockingly, two fold. Not far away, dozens of de-ice trucks rest with glycol steam swirling between them, ready to blast snow laden wings, as the planes sit idly with chocked wheels and darkened cockpits.

They are commuters, these motionless captains of airliners, pulled from the sky for weather-related reasons while trying to get either to work or home. They make up the majority of captains in some hubs, pilots who don't live where they work. They spend huge amounts of time being invisible, either by sitting on planes, or sitting in hotel rooms. Normally they would demand accountability for delays, because every delay cuts directly into their tiny amount of time at home, but they have succumbed to the reality of their being stuck—for a while at least—for they know when they have been beaten. So they sit in uncharacteristic relaxation this night, and pass the time with colleagues, a rare occurrence for them, that people who work among peers take for granted.

"Well, just the other day," the captain from Kentucky says, "I was flying old 'Patches' down to Dallas when my FO noticed that number two'd lost all her oil."

"Which one's Patches?"

"The oldest '73 on the line, the one, if you look close enough, has aluminum patches all over her skin from years of hangar rash."

"What'd ya do?" says another.

"Well, 'Skinner Back Daddy Rabbit,' I say, we let it go until the pressure dances around a little and shut her down right then and there."

"I heard that," says the captain from South Carolina. "Something about a broken starter?"

"Yeah, sure enough, we diverted to Tulsa…drifted down from 33,000 feet, and had her fixed, no problem. Had Patches up in the air again in two hours."

"-ell I'll be. Those boys know their stuff in Tulsa."

"Sounds like you fellows followed the rule of the 6 'P's,'" says the captain from Fort Meyers.

"I heard that," says the captain from South Carolina. "Piss Poor Planning ensures Piss Poor Performance. Or maybe it's the other way around, I always forget. Sounds like you had a good plan…to go into Tulsa."

"It was the end of a four day trip of course. You know everything always happens at the end of a four day trip."

"I heard that. I can hardly stand myself after a four day trip."

"Neither can we, Jack." They laugh.

Sounds mix together in the background: the television replaying news of the blizzard; snow tinkling against the window as if someone had thrown a fistful of sand against it; and a diesel engine hums just beyond, a vacant de-ice truck burning fuel just to keep warm. A younger first officer sits far from the group, contentedly engaged with the sports section of a newspaper, and accepting the unspoken rule of banishment for not enough rank. The center of activity is the table and the men who, by the nature of what they do, cannot help having monolithic personalities.

"Aren't you about ready to retire?" says the captain from Fort Meyers.

"Don't say that God awful word."

"I imagine you are only a year or two away. You got anything planned to do with your spare time?"

"I'll need to work judging by the way everybody's pension is getting zapped…that and an ex-wife or two will put a man in the poor farm after years of servitude. Just don't seem right. The worst part is, I'll be losing the only mistress I ever had…that big aluminum one sitting out there under a foot of snow."

The table is silent as each man agrees. *She* is their only other real love—dependable, beautiful, but unforgiving. They recognize how command changed their personality over time, forced them to believe that though they must accept input from others, they are the ultimate decision makers, because they are ultimately responsible. And since they must maintain control in all cases in flight, only a superman can turn off this trait on the ground, on a whim, a trait that only a super wife can live with for very long—only a super wife could command the house for a few days while her commuter was gone and relinquish command to "the captain" when he returned. They recognize this. They also recognize the implausibility of finding such a flesh and blood woman in a lifetime.

Then they think about their ever-vanishing retirements after years of service, and the way the pilot's pensions are one of the first things eliminated in times of severe need, because they seem so large compared to those who chose vocations with less risk and responsibility. They think about how likely it is to change companies in the volatile airline business, have retirement savings wiped clean, and start at the bottom of the pay scale more than once in a career. Then they think that the odds of being able to retire at sixty, the mandatory retirement age for pilots, with enough savings to actually do it, are very slim.

"You'll just have to get used to Tearing Off Yourself a Slab of Moose Jaw once in a while, that's all," says the captain from Kentucky, lightening the mood.

They nod in agreement, though no one understands what he said.

"If I play my cards right," says another, "I will retire without ever meeting the chief pilot…What's his name?"

"I forget."

"Now that's real L.P.—Low Profile. Flying under the radar. That's just how they like it too. No see-um, no problem."

"Ours is not to reason why, ours is just to do and fly."

"Something like that." They nod.

The snow continues to fall. A man looks at his watch. Just above, in the corridors and gates of the concourse, weary travelers begin bunching up their carry-on bags to form pillows in darkened corners. People lay uncomfortably in seats designed to keep them from doing exactly that, while forcing themselves to not hear the loud conversations from cell phone users. "Cancelled, cancelled, cancelled—all the flights are cancelled!" one says.

"Our ride to the hotel should be here any minute," says the captain from Fort Meyers.

"I'm all about done with this chinwag, anyway."

"I guess it's time."

Each man pulls on his overcoat and slips the buttons through the holes, snugging them up tightly to their chins. Then, one by one, they place their hats with the silver scrambled eggs on the brims on their heads, and amazingly, grab the correct but identical rolling, black suitcase. They slog up the stairs to the upper concourse level and walk by rows of tired and frustrated travelers who plead with their eyes to get them out of there. But their eyes never meet.

Somewhere Over Iowa

The alarm clock screams in the early morning darkness. Alone in her bed, Collette carefully reaches toward the clock, fumbles for the off switch, and silences it. She rarely uses the clock to wake anymore. She rarely has reason to get up so early in her later years and is momentarily lost in the blackness of her bedroom. Her small dog, Kassie, shakes the sleep from her own body, jiggling the tags on her collar and begins to pant, wondering why their routine has changed.

Collette turns on her bedside light, sits up, and rubs bony fingers under her momentarily blinded eyes, and then puts on a pair of glasses. She thinks she isn't as young as she used to be, and contemplates turning the light off and rolling back under the covers of her warm bed and just sleeping the rest of the morning away. But this morning, she cannot sleep. There are few things that happen in her life anymore that make her heart skip as this does, so she rolls her legs off the bed, her knees sparking with arthritis, places her feet on the floor, and stretches. Her flannel nightgown gathers, wrinkled against her body; the bones in her wrists and spine pop and some pain is relieved. The heater kicks on.

"C'mon girl, let's make some coffee," she says in a French accent to Kassie, who is game to try anything, especially if it means going to the kitchen earlier than usual. She walks toward the kitchen in the dim illumination of her bedside light, while pulling on a robe. As she passes a window by the table, she notes the number of stars in the night sky, and how the nearly full moon illuminates the beautiful snow on the ground. She turns on the kitchen light, and looks at the clock, which reads ten after four. She still has time.

She presses the brew button on the coffee maker. It quickly begins to gurgle, filling the kitchen with the woody scent of French Roast. As she waits, she takes a seat at the table by the window, and Kassie sits patiently by her dog bowl. Her house is the only house on Fourteenth Street, one of only a few houses in Coralville that has a bright light shining in a window so early.

"Okay, just over the Cathedral Range there, do you see it?"

"EL Capitan?"

"No, Half Dome, the big, gray rock with the steep ledge. That's all part of it."

"And just to the right of that, a tiny ribbon of white...right there."

"Yosemite Falls, I'm pretty sure."

I lean as far into the windscreen as I can. The Boeing cockpit seems more cramped than usual, especially after sitting in it for nearly five hours, as the snow-covered range of trees and crevasses unfurls beneath us.

"It's beautiful, isn't it?"

We are both mesmerized, watching from a viewpoint that few people have from a few thousand feet above. Those on the ground, no matter how far they hike, no matter how high a mountain they climb, could never know the vastness and magnificence of what we are paid to see this fine day. And it is magnificent. Broken layers of cloud emptied into the western slope of the Rocky Mountains. They were part of a snowstorm that sucked the haze from everywhere west of there giving us perfect, unobstructed, visibility once crossing west of Grand Junction. Utah was clean and crisp, Nevada, an infinite desert with hundreds of miles between dusty towns—scattered below us under a cobalt blue sky.

Air traffic control directs us back to the northwest, toward little settlements with names like Buck Meadows, Moccasin, and Chinese Camp, and then past the snow-capped crags of the Sierras behind us as we glide over the great Stockton valley.

We see San Francisco, nestled on the thumb of a claw of humanity surrounding San Francisco Bay. We can easily make out the nubs of buildings in the distance, the Transamerica Pyramid, and wharfs along the Embarcadero from fifty miles away. Where the thumb and index finger of the claw merge lays the city of San Jose, Oakland being the index finger itself. Approach Control clears us the "FMS Bridge Visual RNAV approach," which takes us just north of San Jose, and we pass over the lower bay, make our turn toward the Dumbarton Bridge, and ease the throttles back, add some flaps.

The main landing runways aim to the west, 28Left and Right, and are close together. Not only do we avoid numerous airliners drifting in and out of the three major airports in the Bay area, San Jose, Oakland and SFO, we must also watch the merging Southwest 737 from our left, also landing at San Francisco. We are for the right side and he for the left.

"I don't like their new paint job."

The 737 gradually swells in the captain's side window, appearing to be on a collision course with us, as we converge toward the runways.

"Do you suppose he sees us?"

"How could he not?"

San Franciscans are used to the sight of a large airplane looming next to them on final to their airport. It is a normal occurrence necessitated by the demand of hundreds of flights through their sky every hour.

"No matter how often we fly in here you never get used to being so close to another airliner. It's as if we are in formation."

"I've seen looser."

I fly to the right of our final approach course to 28R just to ensure that we don't bump each other on the way in. The captain doesn't seem to mind, though he pretends to read the checklist through the window of the competitor's plane.

"Okay, slow it up, we're catching him."

"Gear, flaps, down, checklist complete."

We are just behind and to the right of Southwest. The two runways inch toward our noses, he is definitely for the left now, we for the right, still. We buffet slightly in his wake, but nothing significant. The city is just beyond the airport, and I can see the orange, Golden Gate just beyond it. Three container ships churn away to the east and a flock of seagulls make crazed maneuvers just above us as if they had never figured on a jet plane in this neck of the woods. No Kamikaze's today, thankfully. The water below us seems quite close, green and full of ripples, but our altimeter claims we are just fine. Our brother, Southwest, leaves a smoky bounce cloud and I suppress a laugh, then it's my turn as we float over approach lights pricking out of the water. I hold it, hold it, hold it off, and then...it could've been worse—full reverse.

12:00 noon.

The hotel is a short ten-minute van ride from the airport, and though the sun is ablaze overhead, my body vibrates with a fatigue caused by a month of red-eye flights. The bed is inviting. I do what I can to stay awake. I pace, I watch an autopsy on cable, I eat the biggest burrito I ever saw, I make a special telephone call, but by three in the afternoon my face is nuzzled deep between two pillows that smell faintly like dirty feet. The sun inches below the horizon. A far off vacuum cleaner eventually silences.

Too soon I awake, dizzy, thinking I am in my own bed at home as the telephone rings.

"This is your wake-up call. Good morning," the recording says. In the blackness, my clock reads nine at night. I turn on the light. I get up and look in the mirror.

They don't call them "red-eyes" for nothing.

I take the elevator to the lobby and flip the room card on the desk. A pretty hotel clerk smiles a "Thank you."

"Excuse me?" she says.

"Yes?"

"You're a pilot, right?"

I look down at my black jacket with the stripes on the sleeves, wings over my left pectoral, I'm also wearing my hat with another set of wings on them too. I can't imagine appearing to be anyone else, but sometimes to others we pass as forest rangers, policemen and more often than I care to admit, curbside baggage porters.

"Sure."

"I've been meaning to ask, how do you see at night? Like, in the dark, way up high. Do you have headlights?"

I look around. There are other people standing nearby who can plainly hear her question that seem to lean in close to hear my response, but their heads are turned as if trying not to make eye contact. Either they appear baffled by the question, as simple as it is, or they genuinely wonder themselves. Of course what benefit would headlights be at 41,000 feet, at night with nothing from which to reflect?

"Well, we have instruments that tell us where we are. We don't have headlights per se, but we have landing lights for landing. We see nothing but blackness out of the windows at night most of the time," I say smoothly.

"Yes," she says, "I traveled once at night and I know about those instru-ment thingys, but how do you *see* way up there without headlights?"

A man chuckles, I look for relief, but find none.

"Well—"

"Van's here, you don't want to be late to Detroit tonight, do you?" my captain calls from the revolving door.

"I'll let you know when I figure out the answer," I say to her and wink. "See you Wednesday."

The van ride is quick. My captain didn't sleep well. I can tell by his silence. One or two of our flight attendants slept.

Late at night there are few lines at security—a good reason to travel then, because the airport is not a bustling place. Souvenir shops are gated and dark. It seems that more maintenance workers empty trash bins and clean floors than the number of people milling about. The floors are spo-radically dotted with people curled on the floor feigning sleep—maybe waiting for us.

I like this time. I like feeling far from the command of a wakeful world. The airplane is all ours but for a drowsy dispatcher two thousand miles away perhaps reading a folded newspaper by his side. Forget about any boss, or owner, or president—they are adrift in their own dreamy state. We are awake, coherent and living.

We push and I comment on how much I like Hawaiian Airlines' new paint job. The woman on the tail is more seductive looking than the previ-ous one, and I wouldn't mind having one like her myself someday.

"Looks better than Alaska's, they put the Elephant Woman on their tail," he says.

They give us the Quiet Two departure.

Very soon we are cleared for take-off and thump down runway 1Right. Aircraft 1272 pulls easily into the air. I love this plane; I feel her power, she's so very agile. We climb as if flowing through a dream of twinkling lights, blasting in blackness over the bay, and turn to the left. A quieter San Fran-cisco winks past. We bank to the right and look down upon Oakland and are then released eastbound, back toward the Sierras. My partner stares straight ahead. I can't believe his eyes are still open, but they are. Once the autopilot is on, the plane pretty much takes care of itself, nary a gauge quivers, nary a control moves except in tiny increments to correct for brief puffs.

Solitude and rigid controls only last for an hour until, gradually at first, the throttles mysteriously creep back an inch, and then slowly forward an inch as we pierce mountain wave. At first the wave is light, and the throttles keep a constant airspeed through the up and down drafts of the wave by inching forward and aft. But, by Delta Utah (DTA) the auto throttles can't keep up and the overspeed warning sounds. Throttles come to the aft stop. The downdraft comes, throttles go to the full Max setting, airspeed drags and then catches up gradually.

"Moderate wave tonight," my captain perks up. He manually adjusts the throttles until the wave subsides a little bit, and then clicks the auto throttles back on. They move eerily by themselves, forward and back, forward and back, for the next hour until we reach Scottsbluff, Nebraska (BFF) and then the throttles contentedly find a happy place and stay put.

I tinker with the flight management computer, play with arrival times, slow our speed to hit my mark just when I hope to. Throttles come back a little once again. We chat about our lives for a while. Then the lateness settles in and our eyes sting. We stare ahead. I finger the cold handle in front of my window, cold but the heated windshield is warm, and I begin to get antsy. We have another half hour until I flip my switches on. I can see the waypoint inch nearer on my map display, and am thankful for the stars above and even more for the ones on the ground. There are many more of them on the ground this night, thanks to a cold front that moved through earlier in the day.

"I'll hit the head now. Would you like anything while I'm up?"

"No thanks," he says.

I unbuckle, note the time, and leave the cockpit.

The cabin is very dark. Our load is light tonight and almost everybody is asleep. They look dead, some of them with mouths full open in a typical death mask way, I think, because no one would have their face like that unless they were dead, completely unaware of how disturbing they look. The cabin smells of bad breath and humanly excreted gas and all the things that people do, unaware, while they sleep. I enter the lavatory and relieve myself, and then return to the darkened cockpit. From inside, the cockpit seems darker than earlier as my eyes readjust, and I take my seat in front of the controls again.

Soon, I think.

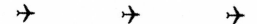

At 4:25, Collette takes another sip of cream-brown coffee and places the cup neatly on a saucer. Through the window, its nine panes dulled by a year of dust, she sees a splatter of dim stars above. Her heart sinks as the kitchen clock ticks past 4:28 and nothing has changed, no stars move, none blink. The sky, in its ever mocking tendency, aims to spoil her morning yet again. Her bed was so warm, so comfortable, so inviting earlier. She wonders if she should have just turned over after shutting off the alarm and drifted off to sleep again. But there she sits fully awake at the kitchen table, as she will stay for the rest of the day. Perhaps there is something good on television, something to get her mind off of the lonely feeling that engulfs her.

Perhaps. Perhaps before succumbing to the TV she can have just a little peek out the front door. But it is so cold outside, so bitter cold. Wearing only slippers and a flannel robe over her flannel nightgown, she opens the front door, stands on the wooden stoop and curses—in ladylike fashion—at the biting cold air that pricks her face. The Iowa night is awash in thousands of stars above, many more than she could see from the kitchen window. Her lower jaw vibrates uncontrollably and her upper chest shivers, and she knows she is crazy standing out on her front stoop so early in the morning, crazy for only a minute and she will go back inside. Kassie claws gently at the front door wanting to come outside and join her.

But then…maybe, can it be? One *does* move, one tiny little star. It is almost overhead, beyond the mall, more over I-80 in the northern sky than she thinks it should have been. She rubs her right eye and adjusts her glasses. Yes, that can be him.

Slowly she raises her right hand. Once it is to the height of her cheek she twiddles her fingers in the direction of the star.

"Good morning, mon bon garçon, my boy," she whispers.

And the dim little light moving across the sky suddenly bursts bright white as every light on the 737 flashes on, as though it had a hundred headlights. She gasps. A delicate smile forms on her quivering lips. For a moment, the chill disappears, and her loneliness is gone, long gone. Then the child whom she once held in her arms so long ago, but now rarely sees, floats silently away at the controls of the big flying machine, high into the night.

PART II

YOUTH

Baseball Backstop

It was over thirty years ago that I lived in Crystal Lake, a town indeed named after a pleasant little lake surrounded by mature oaks and the nicest, moss-laden, brick homes in northern Illinois. It was a time when children outnumbered adults, when a family was prosperous if they had only one car, and traffic jams were only a problem in the heart of Chicago itself. And it seemed as though the few traffic lights that were in town never stayed red long enough to cause a parent to mumble, frustrated, particularly since once entering the town it was only a minute or two before they were home, parked in their own driveway. As people learned about the pleasant quaintness of Crystal Lake, houses sprang up in large developments on the outskirts of the town, like rubber stamped boxes filled with three bedrooms and a bath.

A boy could explore beyond the settlements, in the weed choked creeks and odd corners of neglected farmland for most of the hours in the day, learning the real lessons of life at his own pace. Unlike today, it wasn't necessary for a mother to know his whereabouts every moment, for there was no serious crime, no perverted intentions for young children. And, because there were so many children around, they often organized themselves, without the direction of a parent, into groups of soldiers, or cowboys, or sports teams, and played, usually peacefully, during the day. When dinner was ready, one could hear mothers from almost every front porch calling her offspring to return from the world to eat. One by one, in the late afternoon, I could hear my friend's names called seemingly for miles from the cupped hands of their young mothers standing on front stoops.

Like most country schools, ours had a large, grassy playground with ball fields and tetherball poles, swing sets and monkey bars. In the summer months, when the school's corridors were dark and quiet, it seemed wrong to let this play space go to waste, no matter its proximity to the dreaded learning center, so frequently, and far beyond the tentacles of the fourth grade, groups of children gathered to swing and hit baseballs in the field, fight and make up.

The backstop had been erected just behind home plate to keep spectators from getting beaned by wild pitches or the ineptness of an eight-year-old catcher. It was three-sided, a wide, chain linked box around home plate and slanted upward toward the outfield in a giant, fifteen-foot high wedge. Though no adult would allow it if they knew, we occasionally climbed up the back of it and lay on the slanted top overlooking our teammates swinging wildly at unpredictable balls.

There were only a few of us at the ball field on that sweltering, summer afternoon. Our day of discovering along the creek and finding treasures in the junkyard had put upon us an overwhelming sense of exhaustion. Two of us climbed to the top of the backstop and watched the others swing, but rarely connect with the ball, and we laid comfortably up there, dreaming of a world beyond our little town on our giant hammock of cyclone fence. My chin rested on the tops of my crossed arms as I listened to cicadas buzz in the nearby poplars as I nearly fell asleep there, fifteen feet above the others. Like clockwork, when the sun began its sour glow a few inches above the horizon, the moms started their nightly ritual of calling children just as a farmer calls pigs. My friend with the bat aims his walk for home, dragging the bat behind him, hearing the melodic song of his name, "Jaaaaames," soon to be followed by another, and then the third swore he'd heard his name called and ran to catch up.

Eventually, my other friend and I were the only two souls on the playground, and his head perked at the sound of his own mother's voice from far off.

"That's for me," he said, and pulled himself in a miraculous way over the top of the structure and hung by his hands, his feet dangled nearly ten feet off the ground. He then let go and contacted the earth with a 'thunk' of dirty tennis shoes. After brushing the dust from his pants, he yelled, "See you tomorrow!" and ran off toward his dinner.

Solitude is not what most boys cherish. From my perch, I could see the depths of the grassy park, a swing slowly wandered about its chains, a leaf tumbled from the heights of a dying maple, and the slide stood like a lonely monument to a thousand childhood memories. My name was called somewhere I was sure, but my mother's voice didn't have the punch that other's mother's voices did, so I decided it was my turn to head for home. I glanced over the edge. The height of the top of the backstop was magnified without my friends nearby. To go backward down the fence-wire was more nerve racking than forward, so I succumbed to the idea that I must go forward. I eased my body closer to the edge. The metal was cold. Part of the fence edge was sharp. I positioned my hands awkwardly to grab a tight hold with sweaty palms. I could feel my heart race and I tried not to look down. Until faced with it myself, I didn't fully appreciate my friend's mastery of physics. One knee over…how did one do it this gracefully? I held on tight. And with one firm push, I threw my leg over the edge, closed my eyes, and dropped my other leg.

Something was amiss. Something was terribly wrong. I was nearly strangled as my entire weight was held by my shirt caught in the fence wire at the top of the backstop. Though I planned a graceful dangle while holding on with strong hands, a short dangle until I got my bearings before dropping directly on bent legs, I hung there perilously, powerless.

I took a hand off the rail and pulled exasperatedly at the knot. I panicked. I yanked at it, I prodded it, but I didn't have the strength to free myself. I was overcome with fear. My collar was within inches of choking the life out of me, yet if it tore, I would fall farther than my friend having not carefully hung from outstretched arms, farther onto a hard, packed earth from unready legs. To break my neck in an uncontrolled fall seemed the highest probability. So I hung from high above as the sun eased lower in the sky, as my mother wondered where I was…Just me there as though I was the only boy alive in the world, me and a tiny blip high above, a silver dot pulling a bridal train of a contrail against an azure sky.

But that was long ago. We are in Las Vegas, Nevada, rolling slowly in a right turn onto the long, west facing runway. It is long as all runways are in the high desert. Long, because the air is thin when it is hot and even thinner when it is a high altitude airport. A plane loaded to the gills with people who hoped to win, almost in desperation, what life never gave them through hard work, also needs every inch of available runway. And an airplane like the 737-800 needs that much more runway because, though it is powerful compared to earlier propliners, it has the same engines and wings as the sporty little–700, but a much longer fuselage and a much higher take off weight. Additionally, we have to be careful because it is so long that the tail has a habit of scraping the ground on take-off and landing if a pilot isn't on his best behavior in such phases. So in an effort to disallow any tail scraping of any stretched fuselage, engineers added a few knots of airspeed to the rotate speed, thereby also adding the need for a lengthier runway. But the increased speed for rotation off a runway can only be a finite amount, because there is the added problem of nearing the maximum tire speed, a speed at which the tire blows to shreds—another conundrum of the physics of man-powered flight.

The man I am flying with is near his mandatory retirement age. He is a rare one who lives to make people laugh, often telling the same joke in my presence numerous times to other people who may have missed out on a possible chuckle. I chuckle always, because it is a rare man who makes the effort to spread humor and he should be at least honored for his forthright attempts, and I will miss him when he goes.

Las Vegas tower clears us for take off. My captain slowly pushes the throttles up and the engines spool evenly to 40 percent power, causing the wing tips to shudder with the churning of our engines. He then pushes the throttles up further to 70 percent and depresses the auto throttle switches with an assured index finger, which allows the throttles to go even farther forward to squeeze the maximum amount of thrust out of our engines. Though they roar behind us, a man-made thunder, it is noticeably quieter than in other 737's, because we sit so much farther forward of them in the stretched fuselage.

He releases the brakes and we slowly gain speed on what looks to be a never-ending runway. The nose wheel thumps rhythmically along the centerline lights until he finds the painted line, and though it is normal for this airplane on this day to be pig-like, it is obvious that our acceleration rate is hindered due to the aforementioned elements. The airspeed indicator protests with a nudging needle but continues its slow wind toward our predetermined speed, the speed at which we become airborne. I look ahead and notice how the adobe-brown Spring Mountains rise in the distance ahead of us underneath the crisp, unobscured blue-ness of Nevada skies.

It is a race, a race between our creeping airspeed needle toward the rotate speed and the end of the paved runway. It is as though we are driving cars speeding toward one another in a game of chicken, trying to see who loses his nerve first and calls it quits before a catastrophe. But this is normal in an airline pilot's life I have learned. One must have faith in the gifted men who designed and built the plane, faith that it will actually fly before we run out of runway and become shredded bits of aluminum in the quickly nearing badlands. It is a faith that, I must confess, I don't always feel.

"Vee-one," I call, which is our point of *no reject* speed. "Rotate."

He pulls gently at first and our nose wheel finds the air. There is a barely audible "thop" from the cabin and then the main wheels become airborne as well.

"Positive rate…Gear up," he calls.

The rows of peculiar looking buildings drift off to my right as we climb along the published departure in a graceful left turn. With the sun easing down behind us, we cross north of the majestic walls of the Hoover Dam, then over the glistening stillness of Lake Mead. My captain's finger finds the button that energizes the autopilot and we sit back and watch as desert turns to jagged terrain, and think about where we would build our perfect retirement cabin among the secluded western landscape.

"The tower needs you to contact them on another radio," the departure controller says.

Odd, I think. He just switched us to departure. Now what could he want?

"Yes, I'm glad I caught you," says the tower controller after we switch back, "the aircraft that departed just after you said they saw tire shreds all over the runway. It appears that you blew a tire on take off."

"Thank you," I reply, looking over at my captain, as all copilots do, trying to find an answer in his eyes. He looks thoughtfully straight ahead, probably thinking that it would have been better to have this happen a few days after his retirement.

There I was, I thought, hanging from the backstop again. I am in the air, same as then, dangling over unsure legs.

He quizzes the controller: "How much rubber did you find?"

"It's hard to tell…at least a tire," the controller replies. "Are you planning on returning?"

"Our weight?" he says to me.

"Too heavy right now."

And then he asks me, "Do you see any drop in hydraulic quantity?"

Good thought. All of our hydraulic reservoirs, plumbing, and some of our pumps are located right there in the wheel well, inches from the spinning shards of rubber. They could demolish our hydraulic systems as though they were caught in a food processor.

"Quantity seems steady, as is the pressure," I say.

"No." he radios back to the controller, "We'll continue on to New York and think it over a bit."

Some pilots have 20 years of experience and others have one year of it twenty times. I can tell as he runs scenarios in his head that this isn't the first time he was faced with "The Big Question," because the testing of his mettle over the years created a pilot of his caliber. 'At least one tire,' meant a lot of things. It could mean we lost only the cap of a retread, which was practically a non-issue on a dry runway. The loss of a single tire shouldn't be too much of a problem if that is the case, since there is a second one on the same side, but neither of us had ever landed on such diminished rubber before, and there is a concern that a hard landing, especially at our weight, might just blow the good one, if there is one there. It could also mean multiple tires, which means that when the gear comes down we would have a stump of metal pointing directly at the pavement, and the moment we touched down, we would instantly become the brightest cigarette lighter in the world. I wish there was some way to see what we had.

And I remember dangling as a child from my twisted shirt that tightened with every sway of my body during the four lonely hours to New York. It was back then that I learned one of the sacred truths of attaining a long life as an airline pilot, there, so young, so long ago.

As an innocent child, I wanted to panic, to call for help, to give the responsibility for my survival to a capable adult, but there was no one there...no one to rescue me. As I would later learn, there were seldom times that there would be someone able to rescue me in flying anomalies. To panic would be to give up, to succumb to the harsh unfairness of life, and maybe cease existing, I learned. I took a deep breath to calm my nerves. I tightly gripped the top of the backstop with my left hand and carefully unknotted my shirt from the twisted metal end of the fence-wire with my right. I did this methodically knowing that at any second my shirt could release me to drop hard onto the packed earth. I felt every give of the fabric. I listened intently to the sound of the bending metal wire. I paid no heed to the blood running down my fingers, being cut in the process. I became one with the problem, lifting in directions that were contrary to my first impression. And in time, the fence-wire released me. I dangled from one arm before letting go, and dropped awkwardly to the earth—unscratched.

The captain looked at me.

"I guess we have a job to do," he said. And we put in motion a system that was designed to have the greatest possibility for success. We called upon the greatest minds in our maintenance department to determine how best to overcome the worst-case scenario. We made mental calculations on the amount of rubber found on the runway to determine how much we probably lost. We had emergency personnel stand-by at our destination airport and burned what fuel we could along the way—just in case. We brought some of the girls up front to discuss at length what happened and what they could do to prepare themselves for an awkward landing. And we informed the passengers that though we did not expect anything out of the ordinary they might see a fire truck or two near us on landing, as a precaution.

As the trip waned on, we neared the runway for landing. The ground, contrary to its ever-unforgiving tendency, reached up and kissed our good tires so gently that I have yet to experience a more gentle, eventless, landing.

It was not a moonwalk, nor a miracle, by most standards. But it was still one of the hundreds of examples, lived and exhibited daily by pilots like ourselves, of our mastery of flight.

We did not "conquer the air" when Wilbur and Orville Wright created their flying machine. We conquer it daily, hourly, minutely, by our perseverance and steadfastness in "figuring out a way" to fly within the confines and loopholes of physics.

The Legend of The Tunnel

The sky consists of good and evil and not much in between. Any aviator knows intimately the joys it brings: the sun radiating warmth upon a face in the late afternoon; floating on sturdy wings over ripened countryside; playing peek-a-boo with colossal cumulous dumplings. But alas, one who has spent time aloft knows that the sky has its own temperament, and that it doesn't exist solely for airplanes and pilots, but sometimes for children too.

They were close back then, years ago, when it is said that this terrible thing occurred. James McCollum, an ordinarily airplane obsessed boy whose goal was to eventually fly the line, was thirteen. His little brother, Randy, was nine on the day they found the open sewer down by the creek. After riding their minibike to the far reaches of the field, where the weeds grew tall along the wooded creek and the neighbor's homes were mere white specks off in the distance, they laid it on its side and then climbed the tall metal fence. It wasn't hard for them then, four steps up the fence, a leg over the top, and four steps down. The place had the particular odor of stagnant mildew and mud, as abundant wildlife skittered about. It seemed that everything lived in the pond where it drained. When they stood absolutely still, they could hear the frogs chirp and see minnows flitting in little black masses just below the surface; sharp-tailed sparrows chortled and crows cawed above on the power line that slashed the sky. And, as usual in the summer, there was always the hint of thunder off in the distant, cloud-blackened sky. But they weren't scared. At least they pretended not to be, Randy and James.

"A little help, please," Randy asked, his backpack was caught on the fence and he couldn't drop farther.

"C'mon," James said, climbing up beside and freeing him. He fell to the ground, which wasn't very far, and his foot slipped over the edge causing tiny rocks to drop into the water as he hung on to the fence. There was an uneasy feeling when they were both on the other side, the sewer drain side, once they realized that they were undeniably in unauthorized territory.

"Do you think they will catch us, James?"

"Nobody cares," he said. Randy worried too much, the result of being such a timid boy.

They walked along the edge of the pond, Randy wearing the backpack filled with their provisions like James's personal human mule, as water trickled from the sewer into the pond, then from the pond into the creek. A frog splashed into the water startling Randy, and James laughed.

"Okay, give me a hand here," he said, holding the fence and his hand while stretching a leg over to the concrete tunnel. He touched it with his toe, just barely, and pulled Randy over. Then they both stood on top of it, the five-foot tall sewer drain.

They were two kings of the earth standing there. The only two boys on earth, or so it seemed, commanding every whim without regard for trespassing laws and rules, and the kind of sense that wasn't obviously common. Though they could hear the crows above, the lack of any wind made James feel more alone for some reason, as if the quietness became a barrier between them and civilization. Somewhere the sun shone, but not there, for all they could see was gray above, sometimes light, but mostly dark gray, especially toward the treatment plant. The sky rumbled, then even the birds became silent.

James lowered himself to his stomach and pushed himself over the rim, then dropped his feet into the trickling water on the floor of the big pipe. The sound echoed like rhythmic taps deep into the blackness, and then Randy dropped beside him.

"Hellooo!" he yelled through cupped hands, and a dozen frozen 'hellooos' welcomed them.

"James, this is too scary for me…" 'scary for me…, scary for me…, scary for me…, scary for me,' echoed into silence.

"You're joking," James said, punching his arm. "This is the great adventure we've been planning for a week…pulling the manhole cover cockeyed at the park with Dad's tire iron, figuring the distance. You aren't going to back out of this now, are you?"

"But, still…"

"Forget it. We have flashlights. We'll be okay. We'll just walk it as far as we can until we find the opening at the park, then turn around."

He let out a lungful of air and looked into the blackness.

"Here." He turned him around, opened his backpack and took out two flashlights that he borrowed from their mother's pantry. "This one's yours, I have this other one. Turn it on." They both clicked on their lights.

The two roving cones of light revealed murky walls covered in a green slime that grew up the sides to just above their heads. A little stream sparkled along the floor of the pipe.

"What's that smell?"

"Whatever this sludge is," James said wiping it with his shoe, "it's all the grunge that washes through the town. It flows through here right into the pond. It sorta smells like sewage."

His light flickered out as he moved it and he gasped. Their mother was not known for buying top quality things like flashlights or batteries.

"Use mine." It flickered too, but they both worked better after he tapped them with his palm. Then James said, "Let's check it out."

James led the way of course, as Randy stayed right on his heels shining his bright light ahead of them. His fingers clenched his shirt tightly, pinching him.

"Cut it out." He pushed at his hand, but Randy held on.

Their beams frequently crossed, giving him the feeling of vertigo as their lights bent with the curved walls, so one of James's arms stuck out the way a toddler's arms do when they first learn how to walk. Randy felt the same way, though he remained apprehensively silent, clinging to James shirt. They walked slowly at first, stumbling on the curved floor, growing less and less secure as the entrance receded farther behind them. Slowly, the bright round opening gradually faded from being a large, five-foot wide circle of light to a tiny dot behind them. It was their only way out, James surmised, because most other sewer pipes that he was aware of had crossed rebar wired securely to the entrance of them to keep boys such as themselves from venturing in. This one must have been overlooked, it being far away from the houses and surrounded by that fence. Knowing that, he knew that they must not get lost.

Since neither had ever ventured into a drainpipe before, or knew of anyone who had, they were in the blind in many ways. For all they knew, there was only one long pipe that led through the city and not a maze of tunnels with numerous forks along the way. But they were young then and still ignorant of the unforgiving ways of the world.

"It should be no trouble finding the park manhole entrance. With the cover crooked, it should let in a ton of light."

"You think so?" Randy asked.

"It's so black that even the tiniest amount of light should look like a beacon down here."

The sound of dripping water gave them the sense that they were walking toward a dungeon. With each step they took, they could hear drips ahead and drips behind, but otherwise silence between their sloshing feet. The concrete walls were thick, and the slime so all-encompassing, that they muffled the entire outside world.

"How far do we hafta go, James?" Randy asked with the hint of shaking in his voice.

James's light shone straight ahead, revealing only the nearest ten feet of the tunnel. The haze dimmed anything beyond.

"About a mile…it's about a mile to the park. We'll be sure we are at the right spot 'cause that's where I dropped Dad's tire iron."

"Criminy!" he said coming to an abrupt stop. "This is what I was afraid of."

"What?"

His light wandered around a massive black opening—a fork. The stream at their feet came from the fork on the left; the fork on the right was dry.

"Let me into your backpack," he said, turning him around. Reaching in, fumbling through candy bar wrappers and cans of soda pop, he found his compass.

"I'm glad I brought this," he said, opening it up in his palm. "280 degrees…the park is about 280 degrees from the pond—that I know," he said, sounding very pilot-like.

"Which one do we take?"

"Hmm, the fork on the left would point us further south, about 230 degrees, but the one on the right," he said turning, "would make us walk on a bearing of 350 degrees. We'd be farther away from the park if we took the fork on the right, but I just can't be sure, they are both off."

"Let's just turn back and go home. Dad won't miss his tire iron, and we can come up with another way to get into the park," Randy said.

"Wait. Let's just go on a little farther. See, if we follow the path of trickling water we can turn right around and follow it back to the tunnel entrance. It's like leaving a popcorn trail."

Randy said nothing. They walked, step by step into the depths below Crystal Lake, into the seedy grunge of the concrete passage. A web of strings brushed along James's forehead...Roots! He slapped at them with his hand until his flashlight flew from it and hit the concrete floor with a crack of breaking plastic. At once their light reduced by half and a chill went down Randy's spine.

"I'm glad we brought two," James said disappointedly.

The sense of claustrophobia increased in the warm, stagnant air. They walked, sometimes hunched over for balance, sometimes at a near trot, water splashing by water-soaked shoes.

Thunk—Thunk.

"Stop!" James yelled, sloshing to a rigid stance.

He slowly put a finger to his lips and whispered, "Shhhhhhh."

Thunk-Thunk...

Thunk-Thunk...

"Do you hear that?" he said.

"What is it?" Randy whimpered.

*Thunk-Thunk...*A beating, muffled thump, like a faint heartbeat ahead of them. *Thunk-Thunk.* He could hear it in constant rhythmic *thunks*, though at times it stopped all together and their underground world became silent again. For once, James McCollum really could not come up with an answer.

"I dunno."

He urged him on with a nudge of his elbow, still aiming toward the park.

Thunk-Thunk.

"There it was again." Always in two's. It became louder. The more they walked the louder it became. *Thunk-Thunk.*

Thunk-Thunk.

They moved closer to it, *Thunk-Thunk*, and closer, *Thunk-Thunk*, until it became dreadfully loud. It was right above them! James pointed the weakening light toward the roof with his shaking hand and to their amazement there was a hatch atop a vertical pipe leading to the street above. A manhole cover!

"Cars! The cars are driving right over it."

"Is that our opening, James?"

"It ain't ajar, and it's right in the street."

Thunk-Thunk

"I'm guessing that this is the manhole cover near the corner of Coventry and Suffolk. If that's the case, we still have a long way to go."

James was happy with himself. The sound of his voice was very man-like—assured, even though he had butterflies in his own stomach. He felt like a young Chuck Yeager, famous aviator, leading his brother in the nearly pitch black of the town's catacombs to their secret escape route to the park. He knew they'd be a hit when the other junkyard boys heard about their exploration. They could even start a whole society down there eventually, James being president of course, and Randy—he could be the provisions guy, if he could ever get him to come down there again. Who was he kidding? Of course he could.

"Hold the light steady!" he yelled as they continued walking. And for a time neither spoke until Randy broke the silence.

"James?"

"What, little bro?" he said, peering deeply ahead and comparing their course.

"Do you believe in life after death?"

He caught him off guard. He was trying to check the compass needle in the dim light, but couldn't quite make out exactly what course they were taking. He quickly found out that sewer pipes aren't exactly straight at all, they make barely perceptible turns along the way and it seemed they were turning away from the direction of the park.

"Where did that come from?"

"It's just that...you know...ghosts. What are their days like? Do they get up in the morning same as you and me, get a bowl of cereal, and watch television?"

"Well, everyone knows that ghosts never sleep at night. That's when they do all their clanging and thumping around old houses. So, they must just sleep during the day."

"Why old houses and not new houses? And don't they ever get hungry?"

"They like old houses, because there's been a lot of livin' in them. They like places where there are lots of memories. Those would be the poltergeists—I think that's what they call them—and they can't eat nothing because their fingers would slip right through a spoon or fork. Maybe not a knife, though. I guess a ghost could pick up a knife if he had a mind to. Knives must have some sort of density to them for ghosts. That's why most are angry, because they can't eat anything. They're pretty hungry most of the time."

"For people?"

"I suppose."

"And what about skeletons!"

"Skeletons? Why, they just—"

"No! Skeleton! Skeleton!" he said, jumping and pointing with the flashlight, nearly clawing his arm off in the process. The light beam flickered past what appeared to be a little skull with holes for eyes. Its spinal column was still attached, along with the rib cage and one leg, but the skin was long gone. The arms had apparently floated away down the stream.

"What is it?" he asked.

"I don't know," James said, bending down toward it. "It looks like some kind of dog. It's missing its snout though, like it was a bulldog or something. No tail, either."

"Looks like a monkey."

"No, there are no monkeys here. And it's too big to be a cat. The thing must have dropped into a sewer drain and got stuck. Poor little fella."

"S-spooky, James."

They carefully tiptoed around it as the earth shook with thunder.

"Yeah, ss-spooky," he agreed, realizing then that it could have been—no it couldn't have been—a baby! No—it couldn't. He rushed the thought from his mind as they hurried up their pace.

"That park entrance has got to be around here somewhere. Instead of walking all the way back, maybe we can budge the cover open further with the tire iron and just get out there. This is turning out to be more difficult than I thought."

"Yeah, more difficult."

Time stood still. A month of minutes passed as they trudged on up the little stream passing another misleading manhole cover and another fork. James tried desperately to remember where the forks were, and which direction they took, because he knew that a wrong turn would strand them God knows where, for God knows how long. He looked at his watch, noting the further dimming of their flashlight. It had been an hour since they entered the pipe. The air became more stifling the farther they went and he could tell by the increase in Randy's heavy breathing that his asthma was bothering him. But at least it was warmer than it was out by the pond, and more humid, but the lack of a breeze made him sweat. He still couldn't sense danger then, though it was all around them.

"Ka-Boom!" it thundered from directly above, the earth shook, while tiny flashes of light pierced the darkness through dime-sized holes in the cover behind them. Randy screamed.

"Not far! Not far little brother!" James yelled, hoping to console him with his own feigned strength. "We'll just get out at the park, and we should be there soon. If you can just hold on, we'll be out of here in no time."

"We've been walking forever, James. We should have been there by now. Are you sure you know where we are?"

"Yes, yes," he lied. He looked at the compass, which pointed them dead off at 050 degrees. If only he had a map. "Listen, Randy, you've got to trust me. I know what I'm doing."

Quiet returned. He knew they were nowhere near the park entrance. They had walked too far. It never took them that long to walk there above ground. Twenty minutes. Twenty minutes tops is all it should have taken them to get there. Somewhere they must have taken a wrong turn, but James didn't know how that could have happened since he had the compass and he checked it often. He supposed that it was possible that someone could have replaced the manhole cover that he partly opened the day before. Maybe it was one of the ones that they had already walked past, but why then didn't they see the dropped tire iron directly below it? Maybe it was there under the stream where he couldn't see it. Maybe it wasn't. Maybe they never came close! They were lost, and he couldn't say anything to Randy.

Then, to their terror, the flashlight, just as they realized that it was the most important tool that they had, ever so slowly faded to gold...then to brown...then to black...

Randy gasped.

James pounded the little wand with his other hand! Nothing!

Such blackness cannot be fathomed. It was a thick blackness, a stench-laden blackness that only the dead know. James wanted to be dreaming, in bed rising from this nightmare, but as he opened and shut his eyes repeatedly, grasping that there was no difference in vision, he realized that they were now living their own worst nightmare.

James and Randy McCollum stood in the dark, shock gripping their bone-dry throats, hyperventilating the putrid air, grasping hold of each other. How could this be? How could they not have foreseen this?

"Help!" James yelled, and Randy screamed along with him.

But they were far below the surface, miles from vigilant ears, and as from above, all but the most earth shattering sounds were muffled. No one heard them.

Then…faintly at first, they could hear it in the thick silence, a siren, but not of the assistance kind. Neither of them knew what it was at first, but since it was tested once a month they quickly became familiar with the sound. As it turned on the pole somewhere up there, it became louder, then softer again, then louder.

"This isn't the first of the month, is it?" he asked.

"No, I don't think so."

"Tornado!"

Thunder exploded again, filling Randy's entire viscera with panic!

He started crying, which was rare. James hadn't heard him cry in many years, and he was oh-so-thankful that he couldn't see his clenched face. He held on to James's clothes with both hands compressed tight.

He lost it.

"Stop!" he screamed. "We have to get out of here without light. We have no other choice."

But he paid no attention to him and kept on screaming. And then James calmed himself with the thought that they were entirely safe from a tornado down there, even as the siren continued to blow like an air raid warning.

"Where do people go during tornadoes?" he yelled. "They go to their basements! We are safe here, the safest place to be. That thing couldn't touch us here. Nothing can!"

And then he stopped crying.

"Let's just walk back the way we came," James said, and then he realized that in the darkness he couldn't tell which way they had come. They were turned around and disoriented the same way they were when they played *pin the tail on the donkey.*

How? Think!

It was so difficult to free his mind of mortal thoughts. Which way? The wrong way would put them in the condition of the skeleton a few hundred feet back; the right way would be uncertain freedom.

The popcorn trail! That's it! Their way out was the direction of the stream. Of course, he thought.

While holding onto Randy's hand he crouched, dipping his other hand into the little river and held it there for the longest time. Nothing. He swished it around. Nothing. Which way! Must not panic. Must not panic.

"Ka-Boom!" it thundered again. He fell into the stream; water drizzled onto his lips. It's coming from there, he thought…maybe.

"Follow me!" he yelled. Without hesitation, they walked briskly, Randy clinging to James, whimpering.

Seeing nothing but darkness all around, he couldn't tell exactly where *ahead* was. Though he had an arm out feeling for adjustments in their heading, he still could not help but veer slightly against the rounded walls, tripping and diving to the ground with a splash. Randy hung on knowing that his life depended on it. They'd get up, stumble ahead a few more yards, and then fall again in their confusion. While there, James would put his hand to the water and regain the direction to the pond and, he hoped, home. It was more accurate than the compass once he became sensitive to the feeling of trickling water.

As they walked as steadily and methodically as they could, the sound of the siren faded in the distance, but just because they couldn't hear it did not mean that it wasn't roaring its chilling *wow's*. Somewhere out there was that little yellow horn screaming in the wind, turning on the post, and for miles around people were hiding in their homes because of it. Surely their mother would be concerned that her two only sons were somewhere out there, maybe at a friend's house…hopefully at a friend's house. She was probably calling everyone in the book trying to locate them, but she couldn't know that her sons were exactly where she did not want them to be.

A new sound sent a jolt of adrenaline to James' stomach. This new sound didn't automatically cause concern for Randy, but perhaps because he was the oldest, or perhaps because he was the one charged with being responsible for their group, perhaps...that is why James immediately comprehended the severity of the sound. It was a rumble. A rumble like fat tires on a highway; only there was no highway near the town. It rumbled ahead of them, behind them, it rumbled from the left and the right. The rumble was all-invasive, piercing his every thought.

Rain—not the sprinkley kind, or the misty kind, or the pitter-patter of friendly little drops kind. It was the raining down in torrents kind. It was the raining cats and dogs kind of rain. It was what is known as a *frog strangler* kind of rain. Rain! There is no other more dreadful sound than that!

"Run!" James screamed.

"But?"

"That's rain! And the rain from the roofs of every building in town, from every parking lot, from every mile of road, from every muddy yard, runs into the gutters, and runs right into here!"

They charged through the sinister catacombs, falling most of the way. The tiny drips that they heard before were now gushing all around them as if they were in a sinking, depth-charged submarine with a monstrous current flowing through it.

They ran against the slimy walls. They ran on their knees. They ran on their elbows. They ran like dogs. They ran while the water level rose to their knees. They ran though their feet tangled with each other's and their faces burned hard against the concrete. And as the water level rose even more, so did the velocity of the current making it nearly impossible to run at all. They tumbled more than ran. How Randy never let go James could not imagine, but there he hung on to him as though he was a lifeline, a lifeline that sank like a giant stone.

There were no yells for help. There was no distracting reminiscing, just grunts of terror as they tumbled in the blackness in the chest-high river. How quickly that sewer pipe filled! The things they didn't know that they just took for granted. Who would have ever guessed how quickly sewer pipes fill, and how strong the current became.

Why did he ever think that they needed a secret passage to the park? It made no sense to him anymore. How could he have thought this wouldn't happen? Did he never think it would rain again in Illinois? What was his logic? It was maddening for him to think how his mind changed so quickly and completely under different circumstances. What else could this mean? That his every concept, his every understanding of life, those thoughts that are just accepted and taken for granted, may be entirely incorrect under different perspectives? How could it be? James McCollum's very foundation, the basis for every thought in his head was now suspect, was now…crumbling, and they tumbled…tumbled…tumbled like so much fodder from the streets.

Randy! Where was Randy? His hands were empty of him. His shirt floated around his neck untouched by him. He was gone!

"Randy!" James yelled, but there was nothing except the roar of water. "Randy!"

James tumbled at the whim of the rising water, gasping for air as his head found the surface, and with each gasp, he yelled for him and then held his breath to be pulled down again, his arms flailing for control.

"Randy!"

He did not know how much longer he could continue. He did not know if they were going toward the tunnel entrance, the correct tunnel entrance, cleared and without crossed rebar caging their escape. They may be floating down one of the wrong forks that they passed earlier for all he knew, and being stuck against those metal rods, crossing the wrong opening would surely drown them in an instant. All control was lost. He withered with fatigue. He almost didn't care. He just wanted it to end—except, he had to find Randy.

"Randy!" He coughed, the water inches from the roof of the sewer pipe. As he inhaled, his nose ground against the concrete, and he spit blood before being sucked upside down.

"Randy!"

The sky was vicious as lightning scissored from each end of the horizon in constant, strobing flashes. The wind howled through broken branches void of foliage, and stop signs fluttered like paper on a stick. And, though it was still the afternoon the clouds were so fat with precipitation that they resembled charcoal.

Water was everywhere, pressure-washing everything and then charged toward every sewer in town. It was merciless, relentless, all encompassing. Throughout this and in between the growling thunder, the tornado siren screamed its ear-piercing scream.

Just as James was about to fade, just as he was about to give out that groan that one usually emits only once in their lives, he saw through the murky water, he saw for the first time in the last hour, the tingly essence of daylight ahead. The nearer he came to it the less strength he had. He let the water take him there, not fighting it anymore. He let it pull him toward it, that light growing ever stronger. Then, at once, he was engulfed in the outside world again and tossed into the pool with a splash!

He floated there, feeling the mud gently caress his feet, and grass and weeds tangled into his fists, and he pulled at them until he was up along the bank. Free. He was free again, no longer being beaten by his ignorant curiosity. He breathed in the sweet, succulent air of life. Oh, how he would never take for granted again that sweet, delicious air! He sat on the edge of the pond that overflowed with swift moving water, breathing heavily as the rain pelted his eyes. There was a lump in the weeds. At first he disregarded it as merely a rag doll taken from the sewers being deposited there. He did not equate it to any living thing, but as he focused his eyes on it, it became peculiarly familiar looking—the muddy coat, torn blue pants, shoeless feet! Randy!

He bolted into the water again, grasping at the clump of his brother and by only what can be surmised as the strength of ten men he threw him single-handedly up onto the muddy earth. What had he done?

"Randy!"

He shook him though his head bobbled with eyes rolled back. Nothing! He quickly threw him onto his stomach and pushed at his lower back. He pushed and shook, and pushed and shook until a long stream of brown water flowed from his mouth. He coughed and spit and cried, and James McCollum hugged his brother tightly!

Somewhere up there, somewhere beyond the broken sycamore limbs that fell like pixie sticks on the town square, somewhere beyond the exposed plywood of unshingled roofs, somewhere beyond the twisted road signs, in the heaving wind, and rain, and lightning, a big propellered airplane shuddered in the midst of thunder.

A Gift of Belonging

The pilot is old now. Folds of skin circle his once *eagle eyes*, and there are gray tufts where hair once flowed in a youthful mane. He still towers above the average man though, in height and stature, but with a pronounced million-mile slouch that ever increases earthward by the years—no longer reaching for the sky. He is the most important reason why I love aviation, this man named "Unk."

When I decided I wanted to fly airplanes, I was three years old. I am a little ashamed that I can't truthfully say I wanted to be a pilot all of my life, because I don't remember much before the age of three. But since then I have been preoccupied with winged machines, big ones that thundered beyond the horizon of our split-level home in Illinois, northwest of Chicago. Above, then, they were TWA 707's, United's DC 8's, and multitudes of Convairs, Dougs and Lockheeds.

My father met "Unk" in the Air Force. They worked together as supply officers, getting together after work to play cards and Monopoly alongside their wives, burning steaks and drinking wine. Their lives momentarily diverged when Unk was accepted in the flying program, got his wings in Texas, and shipped off to fight the war in Vietnam.

When I was six, just after the sky churned with a rolling Midwest thunderstorm, my mother looked to the sky and said, "Listen to the plane. The storm is over. Pilots fly around storms so it must be gone." And I heard the faint jet-rumble just like thunder echoing off the houses. I believed that one could have been Unk's B-52 heading back from Asia, telling the world below it was safe to go out again. From that point on, I listened for the sound of jet engines during thunderstorms, signaling the end of them, telling me it was okay to go back outside and play. Airplanes told me when it was okay to be out, a signal just as plain and clear as a dinner bell, and I guess I have always equated that to play.

In civilian life, the two men worked for a Chicago based airline, my father being a manager, and Unk, a second officer on the Boeing 727. Weekends were spent merging families, listening to loud jazz music, and playing board games. Most of the children of the combined families played outside, some of them remarking that the music was so loud that it could be heard over a block away, but I stayed inside sitting close to the men as they played chess and commented sarcastically on the immeasurable qualities of cheap wine. Pipes blazed from two vociferous mouths, filling the room with a buttery vanilla scent that I inhaled happily, listening to Unk's stories of the air. Perhaps Unk felt guilty that I had nothing better to do than to sit quietly to the side, though I wasn't bored, so he thrust a pile of his B-52 manuals upon me and set about losing to my father's deadly Knight's forking. At first, I didn't know where to begin. Thumbing through the old, musty, leather binders, I could have sat there just listening in the background to the delicious jazz music and sarcastic chess observations all afternoon, but eventually I became lost in the immense beauty of the beast that is the B-52.

Children never worry about mortgages and food, because it was always there. I couldn't say the same for Unk when he received his first furlough notice in 1970. What else can a pilot do? He isn't qualified to slide into a management position, or an engineer's position; his job is too specific. And though highly trained, he is unqualified to do practically anything except fly metal, not unlike a tank driver or artillery operator in the military—there just is no civilian equivalent. With a wife, four children, a dog named Skippy and a mortgage, Unk changed tires at a Goodyear store to get by. Then, of course, there was the other furlough for two and a half years due to the Arab oil embargo in 1974, and the strike of 1985.

I never noticed any disdain for aviation from Unk, even while bleeding financially during the furloughs and strikes, but maybe my concern for Unk manifested itself in my nightly dreams. The whole neighborhood knew of them—giant machines, zooming through the never-sleeping mind of a young boy. I awoke, often in a sweat, delusional, not recognizing my mother's worried face, still under the spell of the flying behemoths. People would talk, they'd say, "Have you had that dream again? The one you have trouble snapping out of?"

But, just as I outgrew poltergeists, bogeymen and other phantoms of the night, I also said *good-bye* to my last machine with the rat's nest of wires and gauges, darting about my head, coincidentally about the same time that the furlough ended. Then I realized that anything we Americans wish to be is within our grasp. All it takes is ambition and a certain fire in the belly, as Unk had, to accomplish our goal. I learned as I watched him persevere, eventually upgrading to the right seat of the 737, the DC-8, the DC-10.

The chess games between him and my father continued, then in our new home in Denver, not far from the flight training center. We had many visits with Unk, but perhaps the most memorable one was when Unk managed to sneak me in to fly a Boeing 727 simulator late one night on one of his overnights. The smell of wires and worn transformers, and the sound of whirring hydraulic actuators, pumping under the strain of heaving boxes of men about in perceived (and real) anxiety were a flight-obsessed boy's dream. There is no better sensation for a fifteen year old boy than to handle the control wheel of a Boeing jet through taxi, take off, and landing, all under the watchful eye of the master, a man who, with the gentleness of a grandpa, talked me through each unbelievable maneuver. Then of course, the die was cast, my calling set.

My passion continued with trips to the local airport and strolls along the flight line in subsequent years. I looked in every window, caressed every silvery spinner, and sniffed the fuel-scented air as a starving man would a Thanksgiving dinner, as a purring Cessna floated gently upwind, departing for skies yet unknown to me. I passed open hangars revealing greasy mechanics who would stop their wrenching to talk with anyone willing to share their delight. Here is where all are accepted, I thought, and here, at the county airport, is where I will receive my wings.

Young people get wrapped up in their own lives. As we scramble to start our own careers and families, we don't always notice when our elder's dreams fall apart. It came as a surprise to me that Unk's marriage fell apart. Just as devastating, but not as surprising, was that his Klipsh Corner Horn speakers somehow ended their lives simultaneously in a heaping pile of burned rubble. But break-ups are as common as halitosis in a dry cockpit, and I only found out after the scramble, the details of his messy split.

He never forced aviation on me. In fact, he made a point to say that it isn't an easy life. Furloughs and strikes aside, he mentioned the fearful nights of weaving through cumulous towers, questionable landing gear and burping engines. He mentioned the difficulty of noisy hotel rooms, and sick children two thousand miles away, a tearful wife, or the occasional crap-brained captain. He informed me of the dangers because, had he not done so, he would have regretted that I would experience all these things and perhaps give up, disillusioned, never experiencing what flying is really all about. He prepared me.

I hope you know what it's all about. I hope you know what it's like to have transcended from the human world to the flighted world, in utter harmony with the clouds and sky. I hope you have felt the rumble of fifty thousand pounds of thrust surging by the movement of your fingertips. I hope you know what it is to have brought forth, landward, the lives of a hundred or so, safely. The accomplishment is unparalleled. To look back on an airliner, parked safely at the gate because of your own doing, is to see the newly opened eyes of a newborn child, for that bird is you, an extension of your very soul. I hope you know, as I do.

Once I made the majors, I was lucky to have been merely sent to the Pacific during my first furlough. I never had to turn a wrench under a greasy Buick to make my mortgage payment. In comparison, my gauntlet of passage was done in the wee hours over the ocean, sitting sideways, plumbing the panel of a 727, instead of by changing tires. I have always viewed a successful career as a professional airline pilot as traversing a succession of minefields consisting of furloughs, strikes, medical anomalies, and bankruptcies, all of which will undoubtedly surface throughout a career. I knew this before my first solo, thanks to Unk.

But then in 1994, my father died unexpectedly and life became less meaningful. The jazz-filled chess games of my youth were forever filed away in the joy slot of my memory. No more vanilla scented pipe smoke, no more drunken laughter over unbelievable chess forkings, no more Dad. Life seemed monotonous, dreary. Not even flying brought the elation it once had.

One day, I found a box near my front door. It was from "Captain Unk." I cut the tape and peeled open the top, curious why he would send something out of the blue. Inside, a note read: "I was cleaning out my closet and thought you might want these." Twenty years later, I immediately recognized the brown B-52 binders. As I thumbed through the pages, I realized that, though I now am flying from the right seat of a Boeing, I understood then what I understand now: the numbers were inconsequential. The B-52 started it all for me: the long, swept wing; and eight mighty engines; flying in a black and white photo somewhere over the American plains. The graphs and charts, ancient numbered checklists, and torn paper were a gift of belonging.

As the years passed, I sensed a fatherly pride for my accomplishments in aviation from him. We swapped stories of blinding snowstorms, and foggy mornings, and cranky passengers, and cranky airplanes. The Internet has bridged a chasm that previously had separated families forever by geography. Now, we are merely a keystroke away and I write, and send blasphemous chess moves of my own, while asking advice on atypical airliner problems. If an airline pilot had an owner's manual, it would be "Unk" as he has seen, in his thirty years of flying them, nearly everything that came down the pike, and luckily I had access to his treasure of experience.

His last flight was in the winter of 1998, Maui. I was snowed in up in New England, wishing he had just one more trip so that I could ride his jump seat one time. But, before I dug out, his time on the line had run out. Upon return, he quietly unpacked his overnighter, hung up his hat, and bought a small sailboat to command in the twilight of his life.

It is rare that I visit the old aviator, he on the west coast and I on the east. But I did recently. Like most old pilots, he craves command, to soar again. He is an old sled dog, pulled from the traces for the younger, wishing to give his last ounce just to be part of the team, to have worth. He is what he is—a pilot, and once he is no longer, he, in his mind, is just an old man. Pilots don't realize this until it is too late, of course, until the bell tolls its sixtieth time. A sailboat isn't quite the same no matter how hard one's wife pretends to be a trusty copilot.

We sailed one sunny afternoon, Unk and I. I relieved his new wife to become his temporary new copilot. We didn't sail a boat that day, we sailed a Boeing 767. Never before was a little Potter sailboat sailed so smartly on Prineville Reservoir in Oregon. We tacked and jibed with nary a line unraveled. Later, at dinner, as he opened a bottle of claret to celebrate our masterful cruise, he made an introduction to friends: "This young man here was recently promoted to captain," he said proudly, "something I was once, but am no more."

Funny how wrong that sounded coming from the man I epitomized as *the* pilot. Yet, I realized at that moment, in those few words, that the baton had been passed. He poured, and we drank the wine as stories of airliner flying drifted from our mouths until the wee hours of the morning.

Ely's Story

Sandy would be dead in less than two minutes. But at least it would be quick. She could feel the dampness between her fingers and under her palms as her hands gripped the icy steering wheel tightly, jarring it to the right as the little truck tires slipped out of the snow-packed ruts. They dug into the loosened snow as the front of the truck slid to the left and then thumped back into the ruts again, back under control in the way a train track guides the wheels of a wobbly train. She squinted at the pink taillights ahead, her only true indication that she was on a road amid the whiteness of the unexpected blizzard, and hit the accelerator in an attempt to keep them in sight. The back of the truck fishtailed out of the ruts and back into them again in the gusting wind, and all she could think of was that she was damn tired of the snow.

She glanced at her watch and said, "Christ! I should have been at the bank twenty minutes ago."

Highway 30 took a meandering curve down Walnut Hill through central Vermont making the four-lane highway resemble a giant "S" through the patchwork of rolling farmland. In the midst of a scattering of small homes and erect silos that dotted the great white parcels every half mile, and between groves of sugarbush that broke the countryside in a perfect balance of nature and rural commerce, Highway 118 merged into Highway 30 in a gradual "V." Not far from this confluence, an old farmer with a red-checkered, floppy-eared hat stood in front of an open barn door lighting a pipe clenched in his tobacco stained teeth. As he heard rather than watched the highway traffic buzz by his homestead, heard the muffled sound of snow being thrown from tires in the baying wind, he made a mental note that he was glad he didn't have to drive in such weather. Glad also, because if he couldn't see the normally giant snake of vehicles roaring by his house every minute of every day, how could they see each other?

"The damn fools."

The taillights faded ahead. Sandy blinked hard trying to concentrate on what little she could see of them. She reached for the radio knob, taking her concentration away for just a moment to search for soothing music that could calm her already shot nerves.

"Fourteen goddamn more miles."

She looked up quickly. There was nothing but white beyond the whipping wiper blades. She pushed the accelerator frantically with her right foot hoping to catch the little pink taillights, or any semblance of a road, again. As the rear tires spun momentarily, a ghostly blue sedan merged into her from Highway 118. She gasped. Her heart thrust against her chest as she swerved hard to avoid it—swerved in a reflex that normally would be appropriate on a dry road. As she did, the little truck slipped out of the compacted tire track ruts that guided it so perilously.

She rotated the steering wheel wildly to the right, then recklessly to the left, strangled with fear. She pushed hard on the brakes, harder than she had never pushed before, exacerbating the gyrations of the swerving truck. It thumped backwards out of the westbound lane, over the median, sliding three hundred and sixty degrees around. Though the feeling of powerlessness was overwhelming, the act of bouncing over snow-covered grass gave her a sense of relief because, in her mind, there would be no cars on the median. But, because the ground was slick with snow covered ice and the down-slope of Walnut Hill was just enough to allow her sliding to continue beyond her expectations, her fear intensified as the little truck thumped past the median, back onto the opposite side of the highway. It slowly turned and came to a stop facing the most terrifying thing a human could ever imagine.

In the deep whiteness of the blizzard, a gray phantom monolith materialized rapidly in front of her.

She closed her eyes…

…And screamed.

The old man burned the tip of his index finger forgetting to drop the match when he heard the terrible sound. It was the most destructive thing he had ever heard—one loud, short, semi-truck horn followed quickly by the thunder of large chunks of metal ripping. He had heard explosions on television before, but this was far worse, because it was right before him. Something zinged by his head sounding like a stray bullet. Surely not a bullet, he thought, it had to have been glass, or part of a bumper, or a shifter knob. But the collision continued for what seemed an eternity, large chunks toppling end over end from his left to his right—seemingly inches away—hidden in the fog of the blizzard, a pop, a thud, broken glass muffled in the snow, another car horn, more tearing metal, a hiss, another crumpling sound. Then silence. It was as if death became the countryside, death became the world in that tiny corner of Vermont. There were no more car traffic sounds, no tires whirring by as they always had—just the wind, tingles of snowflakes upon his face, and the smell of blood and antifreeze.

"Oh, no!" came the muted sound of a man's voice from the fog by the nearby sugarbush.

The pipe fell from the old man's teeth and dug into the snow.

"Tilly!"

"Tilly!" he yelled, running toward his house, "Tilly, there's been a terrible accident! Call help right away!"

Ellison Sullivan closed the magazine and placed it gently on the table by his bed. He was feeling particularly lonely for some reason, though usually reading the words from the pilot in the magazine gave him a sense of belonging. He had no brothers or sisters; he never knew his grandfather or his father. He had grown up in a house that he and his mother shared with his ailing grandmother. A boy among women, he frequently felt out of place. And being gentle, he was leery of the rough and tumble boys, local simpletons who did not stray from thoughts beyond their rural community. He was more prone to the exotic imaginations of a dead author's written words, which sometimes transformed his bedroom into a giant oaken brigantine trashing upon the churning sea. But mostly, his thoughts were toward the sky, because an airplane could lift him away from the reality of his lonesome world more quickly than a ship.

"Ely, come here darling," his grandmother, Margaret, called. He could tell by the sound of her voice that she was dreadfully serious. He sat up quickly, scratched the base of his neck, and went downstairs to find out what was wrong.

As he approached, he slowed. He had never seen such a solemn look on her face before. She appeared so old, and so worn out, as she dropped the phone on its cradle from frail fingers. Something was terribly wrong. He stood, looking at her, waiting for her to speak, but it was an uncomfortably long pause.

"Your mama...your mama...there was an accident...your mama..." She wiped her nose.

An eternity lay between each of his grandmother's attempted utterances.

"On the way to work..." Margaret suddenly held her breath, forcing the words out. "Your mama died in a car accident on the way to work today."

He let the thought of his grandmother's words float through the morass of his mind as he stared into her weary eyes. Though the whites were pink with the distressed sparkle of hundreds of tiny tear droplets, they were darker than he had remembered, and more beautiful. For the first time, he could see his mother's face in hers, and focused on it as if he could somehow absorb her by memorizing every feature: the little rise in her cheekbones; the flair of her eyebrows—Mother—crooked front tooth, that too. She cleared her nose with a tissue and pulled him to her breast, hugging him tightly. Her tears wet his neck and shoulder as she cried.

He thought he knew the depths of isolation, but before this he could never understand the absoluteness of it, the depth of desperate sadness and loneliness in hearing the tragic news of the death of his soul mate mother. His arms hung stiffly by his side, his back—rigid in the hug—and his right knee shook as though there was an unstoppable motor in his foot. He had a hollow look on his face as though his own life had been extinguished. The words repeated themselves in his mind: "Your mama died in a car accident today."

"Ellison, don't you worry, baby. Everything's going to be all right," his grandmother wept.

"Can I see her?"

For fifteen years, Sandy had been everything to him, the ever-consoling mother for his every need, his best friend, sometimes his only friend. She was always there. Suddenly he became overwhelmed with a sense of guilt for the times that he worried her, took advantage of her, and argued when he should have shut his goddamn mouth.

"I want to see her," he said.

The back door in the kitchen closed quietly followed by footsteps. Others followed up the walk and entered the house, Trish, his cousins, Jason and Matt, and uncle Mike. As they entered, their eyes didn't meet Ely's; none spoke. The looks on their faces held volumes.

"When can I see her?"

"Ely," Margaret said, coughing into one hand and putting her other hand on his shoulder, "You can't see her, dear."

"Why?"

"There's..." she stopped. "She's...too bad off, dear."

She burst into tears and hid her face in her hands. "I'm sorry. God knows I'd rather it'd been me than her."

The house filled with crying mixed with people sobbing that Sandy's life had been taken too abruptly. Mike paced the room while Trish consoled her mother and tried to talk to Ely. Ely pushed away from her and ran to his room, locking himself in.

"Let him be," Mike said.

As a way of gaining control of his world, Ely did what he had done so many times before; he opened up the magazine, and read.

In time, the clouds split like shattered glass, and the pink sky of a waning sun shone through the cracks echoing twilight. The house quieted.

Ely dropped the magazine and stared at a floating Douglas DC-3 in Eastern Airlines colors slowly twirling from a string secured to the ceiling in his room. He laid there for hours, late into the night, unable to sleep while the adults sat at the kitchen table speaking in hushed tones.

The subject strayed from Sandy.

"But, this is the only home he knows," Margaret said, her hands shaking more than usual from her Parkinson's disease.

"You know you are too old to raise a fifteen year old boy," Trish said. "Mike and I will take him, won't we?"

"For Christ sake, this is too early to be speaking about his future. We have to bury his mother the day after tomorrow," said Mike.

"Oh, Jesus, help me. My baby girl is gone," Margaret wept into her hands.

Mike finished the last dregs from a can of beer and squashed it with his fist.

"Just rest assured he's going to be okay. He'll know who his family is, that I can guarantee."

"Mike!"

"What, Trish?"

"I know what you're going to say."

"Look, you remember what split Sandy and Jake up. There's the law and his natural father's got to know."

"Shut-up, damn it. He'll hear you. Don't say another word!" she whispered hoarsely.

"If it was me, I sure as hell would want to know. He should at least be notified; besides, I got the time to do a little investigating."

"Maybe if you'd get off your ass and find a job, you wouldn't!"

"Trish, you know there ain't nothing out there."

"Quiet!" the old woman said. "I've heard enough of this. You are killing me; I'm the one dying now."

Mike pushed his chair away and stood up, leaning forward with his hands on the table. "I know how to contact him. She told us his name, you remember Trish, and I remember it too. He's got to be somewhere...on the Internet."

"I can't talk about this right now. I just can't! Besides, Sandy told us confidentially, Mike."

"Yeah, we were never to tell Ellison when she was alive. Now everything has changed. This is why she told us."

"Ely's been everything to Sandy. We've seen him grow up here. We mustn't confuse the boy. I won't allow it," Margaret said. "This is his home."

"His real father needs to at least be informed. It's the decent thing to do," Mike said.

The old woman stood and walked to the sink, she wiped her face with a dishtowel. "I've heard of this happening to other people. You know, I just never expected..."

"No one did, mama," Trish said.

An uncomfortable pause hung over the room. Mike opened up another can of beer. "I know what to do," he said, taking a long pull.

The memorial service was held in the large, white, Victorian funeral home on the corner of Allen Street. Outside, maple branches hung low with a fresh dose of newly fallen snow that morning, which also covered the crags and imperfections of the town in a soft, downy, blanket of white. It was as if the Snow attended her funeral, a curious child, returning after the tantrum to see what devastation it had wrought. There is beauty to the land, as the sun gleamed through dumpling clouds, reflecting upon the windows of the home, and the cars, and the ice patches on the sidewalk. People filed in from the parking lot, tapped the snow from their shoes, and removed their coats. A gentle piano concerto played faintly from ceiling speakers in the lobby. The smell of roses partially masked the odor of disinfectant and formaldehyde in the unventilated house.

Though Ely sat up front, still in disbelief, denying both consciously and unconsciously, the permanent loss of his mother, he was surprised to see how many people came to pay their last respects to a person, who had on many occasions, showed dislike for almost every one of them. He knew that they were mostly from her job at the main branch of the bank. Maybe they came to verify the end of their troubles, or just grieve for the loss of a person who made them so miserable. Ely knew his mother would never have won a popularity contest in this town. But maybe these mourners were all here thinking, "…But for the Grace of God…" as if sealing her end ensured them continued life. Like the human sacrifices in a "primitive" culture. He hated them all, staring, staring at the floor, the ceiling, the door, and the big, black casket. Old couples sat and stared straight ahead; a few women, dressed in black, cried, and others who looked familiar, people he hadn't seen but once or twice in his early childhood, stood along the rows of filled seats. Some came up to him and held his hand while pretending to hold back tears; some looked at him sympathetically, which made him more uncomfortable; still others wept openly as they hugged him.

"You were everything to her," they kept repeating. Which he felt was supposed to make him feel better, but angered him more than anything. It put pressure on him, the sole joy in her life, to have supplied her with a life fulfilled. And now he would never know if he actually made her life better or was more of a burden. All that he knew was that he loved her more than anything and felt more alone than he could have possibly imagined.

Through the drone of mumbling voices, he kept hearing, "What will happen to him? Who'll take care of Ely?"

The music stopped. A young man holding a book with a ribbon hanging out of it walked to the front of the room. Ely wondered what kind of life experience this man had to give him the authority to send someone to the grave for eternity. He seemed to be too young, his hair was combed too precisely, his skin pink. Nothing about his appearance was offensive, as though all of his personality had been carefully groomed away, like a fastidious dentist. The man cleared his throat, and spoke eloquently, but with a boyish crackle, about the Lord taking away our beloved for grander purposes in some afterlife. His grandmother coughed persistently, the oft-interrupted words that floated about the room had little effect on Ely.

The long train of cars with illuminated headlights followed a Cadillac hearse for a mile down Allen Street. They passed Ely's favorite hot dog stand that was closed during the winter, and the movie theater, and the school that he normally would be attending but for his mother's funeral. They turned the corner into the town cemetery and parked along a dirt road just a few yards from a freshly dug hole in the frozen earth. Then he stood, flanked by his grandmother and Trish, in front of the hole as a small party of men dangled his mother's coffin from down-stretched arms and placed it upon two pea green straps just above it. She wouldn't feel comfortable sleeping, as he imagined, among the hundreds of stranger's tombstones that sprung like rows of rigid columns of little soldiers in formation about the cemetery.

The young minister with the combed hair mumbled some more words about ashes to ashes and dust-to-dust while Ely noticed a small jet plane slashing the sky with a contrail high above. The minister then said something about the world being a better place because of his mother's kindness, though he had never met her, and then closed the book with the ribbon. A woman gave Ely a rose, which he placed carefully on the casket. Then he kissed his fingertips and gently touched the top of it. People slowly walked away in whispers behind black sunglasses, sunglasses hiding either real tears or the lack of them. Some patted him on the back and shoulders. Some said, "If you ever need anything…" And he thanked them all, as he remained standing there, still hearing whispers of "But will happen to Ely?"

Ely returned to his daily routine as quickly as possible, as if denial was the best way for overcoming trauma, a *getting back on one's horse after a fall*, so to speak. It meant that after two days of sitting with, and staring at loved ones on his grandmother's sofa, wondering what to think, he would return to school where he would sit at a small desk among teachers and students and stare at a blackboard and wonder what to think.

A week later, Mike burst into his mother-in-law's kitchen.

"Where's Ely?' he said.

"Still at school," she said. "Why?"

"I've found his father."

She dropped a rag she had been using to wipe silverware, unable to come up with a reply. The words just sat in the base of her throat like tiny rocks that she couldn't choke out. Though she knew it was the right thing to notify Ellison's natural father, she had secretly hoped that he would never be found.

"The Internet is the most amazing thing. I put in the name and approximate location of him fifteen years ago and it spit out five possibilities within an hour. I sent them all cards and he replied. Everet replied. I talked to him today."

"Jesus, Mary and Joseph, Mike, of all the things, this is not something I wanted to deal with."

"We spoke for an hour. He was absolutely floored. She never told him, she never goddamn told him he was a father," Mike said.

"Oh, dear," she collapsed on the chair, "tell me what was said."

"I got to have me a beer."

"You know where they are."

He pulled open the refrigerator and grabbed a can from the bottom shelf. "It's like this," he opened the can and gulped. "He lives in Pennsylvania, and he's married with another kid, and he also moved around a lot with his job. When I told him about Ely, you could have blown him over with a feather."

"What else did he say?"

"Well, I kind of don't want to tell you the next part."

"What? Tell me." She steeled herself for the worst.

"He's coming up here next Tuesday."

"He's coming up here?" She slapped her hands on the table. "That's what I was afraid of. Ely doesn't need this kind of confusion right now. He's obviously depressed and confused. He'll feel he was lied to his whole life."

"He was."

With an hour left to go in math class, Ely found himself unable to concentrate on the teacher's discussion on algebra. On a good day, he could barely understand the concept much less see the correlation in real life terms. It was all he could do to keep from thinking about his mother, as he frequently did, thinking about her there in the cold, dark ground a few miles away from his school, alone. His teacher's voice became a buzz of confusing terms. He needed to get away, to escape from life again and the nonsense of unnecessary thoughts.

When he was sure his teacher couldn't see, he carefully slid his hand into the backpack under his chair and pulled out a copy of Airways magazine. He put it inside his open notebook, making it appear as though he was reading his notes. Then he flipped through the pages until he came to, "Chet Jetzen."

"Take me away, Chet, take me away from this bullshit," he mumbled. This time, just as all the rest, Ely flew. The author's words buoyed him as he described exactly what it felt like to be adrift in a hurling, metal machine. One thousand, five thousand, ten thousand miles away, he brought his readers and their passionate imaginations with him as he flew.

"Ellison, I trust you will be ready for the test on Friday?"

He looked up from the magazine at his teacher's serious gaze and slammed closed his notebook. The magazine dropped to the floor and the classroom roared in laughter at his embarrassment. Moments later the bell rang, ending school for the day.

The regulator clock on his grandmother's living room wall ticked unusually loudly. There was nowhere in the little house that the ticking didn't penetrate: the bedrooms; the bathroom; even if a person stood near the wall in the garage he could hear it. The air was particularly heavy with the incessant, somber ticking and the odor of beer and rose potpourri. Mike and his mother-in-law, Margaret, sat silently on the sofa, waiting. The clock chimed three thirty. There were two thumps on the front porch before the door swung open.

Trish walked in with Jason and Matt, accompanied by a cold blast of air. She dropped her keys into her purse.

"What are you doing here?" Mike grilled Trish.

Margaret moaned.

"That's a fine way to greet your family," Trish replied.

"We're expecting the boy," he said. "You're supposed to be home."

"Home? I came to check in on Mom. What about you? What are you doing here? Besides drinking, of course."

"It's about Ely. I got some big news today," Mike said, lowering the can of beer into his lap.

"I don't believe this."

Someone cleared his throat behind Trish.

Ely stood in the doorway.

"What's up?" Ely asked.

"Hey, Ely."

"Hey, Jason." Ely replied.

His grandmother coughed into her hand. "Your uncle Mike has something to tell you, Ely."

Ely dropped his backpack on the floor by his feet and closed the door behind him.

"Tell me what?" he said, walking towards them. "What now?" he thought to himself, and swallowed hard.

"Please," she said, "sit over here by me, dear."

"Ely…" Mike said. "I had a little telephone visit today."

Trish looked disappointed. "Is it about who I think it is?" she interjected. "Never mind, I don't want to know."

"Yes, as a matter of fact, it is," Mike said.

"C'mon boys, lets go. We don't need to be here for this. Mom…" she said, facing her mother, "I told him not to do this. I don't take any responsibility for any of it. If he wants to screw up this child's life, there's nothing I can do about it. I was going to see if you could watch the boys while I went to the store, but now I've changed my mind."

"Child?" Ely said, feeling like a bothersome liability. Why couldn't they see it was enough for him just to get out of bed these days, drag a toothbrush across his teeth, drape clothes on his back, slog to school, and listen to the gobbledygook flowing from the teacher's mouths without also being tossed around at home like some sort of emotional volleyball?

"I have things to do," Ely said, and went into his room, closing the door. He rolled up a piece of sand paper into a little tube and slid it over the index finger on his right hand. Then he picked up a piece of balsa in the shape of a tiny airplane stabilizer and began rubbing the sandpaper gently over the wood as he thought about his mother. Something was missing. He poured a small amount of glue along the edge of it and secured it to the end of a spine of wood with a piece of tape.

That ought to hold it until the glue is dry.

A five-inch thick stack of Airways magazines sat on a shelf in the headboard of his bed. One day, he thought, he would join the aviators the likes of Chet, in between the pages of the magazine, flying wistfully unshackled from the drudgeries of the earth in giant, wonderful machines. But until then, he lay on his bed and grabbed an old issue…and read the words of his good old friend.

There was a gentle knock on his door.

"Ely?"

"Yes, Grandma?" he said, placing the magazine carefully next to him.

"I'd like to have a talk with you. May I come in?"

"I guess so."

He pulled himself up from his bed, walked to the door and turned the handle. She stood alone, marveling at the boy's room, the poster of a 747 in a steep banking final approach with Hong Kong's skyline behind it on the wall, the mess of wood and papers on his desk, the row of tiny models along the shelf.

"These are wonderful. I never really noticed how detailed your airplanes were. Did you make all of these?" she asked, examining them.

"Most of them," he replied. "Did Mike leave?"

She hesitated. "I asked him to go home with your aunt."

"Oh."

She touched the wing of a red Braniff 727. "This is pretty."

Ely remained silent.

She realized that she was avoiding the reason that she came into his room. She lowered her hand from the delicate model, then walked toward his bed and sat on the edge.

"You know, I never wanted to tell you this before, but your Uncle Mike insisted that you needed to know. Considering how you've been lately, I kind of agree."

"About what?"

Margaret hesitated, thinking about how to carefully word her next statement.

"Your mother was doing okay raising you. She had a plan, you know, back when she was married to Jake. It was a good plan. They were going to raise you in a nice house of their own, have a nice family...maybe have a few other babies. I was so proud of her." She coughed, purging every bit of air from her lungs. "We were all surprised when we found out..."

"Grandma, if this is bad news I don't want to know. I've had enough bad news this month."

"No, dear child, it isn't bad. I thought it was at first and I didn't want you to know; I didn't want anyone to know. I was ashamed of her when I learned the truth. It is what broke her and Jake up back when you were a baby."

"What?"

She cleared her throat preparing herself for what she thought would be the second most serious revelation in the boy's life.

"Mike located your father," she said soberly.

"Jake?"

"No, dear, your real father."

Suddenly Ely's world was crumbling around him again. Real father? How could that be? The man his mother called Jake, the man he didn't remember, because he left before he was two, was the only father he knew. He had a picture of him on the shelf.

"You mean there is somebody else?"

"Yes, child."

"Who is he? Where is he? Is he here? Will I meet him?"

"He wants to meet you."

"Why now? Why does he want to see me now, after all these years?"

His grandmother looked down as she rubbed her two thumbs over her interfolded fingers, and sighed.

"I don't know." Her voice seemed to drift away in time as she continued. "I didn't know that Jake wasn't your father until he left your mother when you were a baby. Your mother asked us never to tell, but now she's gone, and you deserve to know. Maybe you can ask him why he never wrote you, or called you, when you see him."

Ely felt a mixture of anger and deceit. All of a sudden he couldn't trust anybody. He felt so cruelly betrayed by life, why should he trust things now?

"I don't know if I want to ever see him. What about my feelings? Tell him...Tell him to go to hell."

She hugged him, and then stood up.

"If that is what you wish. I'll tell Mike to phone him and tell him you aren't interested."

Six days later, as Ellison walked to school under twisted sugar maples that dusted the undersides of stratus clouds like feathers under a blanket, he heard the northern wind howling, melting into the thunder of an airplane somewhere deep within the sky. He looked up, as all aviators do, momentarily puzzled as he tried to locate its direction, but could not see it as it flew above the clouds. As it neared, he unconsciously tuned his ears to the chord of its engines, their pitch in harmony with the song of flight, a lament to the dreariness of February.

There was something about that plane.

Then he knew without guessing what drifted somewhere above. It came as second nature to a lover of anything with wings and motors. He didn't hear the whiny pitch of Allisons, or the buzz of Garretts, the *who* of CFM's, or the *nay* of the GE—he heard Pratt and Whitneys on a Boeing—and with turbines ever so slightly out of sync.

The park that he passed in the center of town on his way to school is a cemetery in the winter, as was everything, it seemed to him lately. Even the pigeons were extinct from the cold granite monuments to summer heroes, and the bird-songs were replaced by the crackle of falling tree branches in the incessant, cussing wind.

As the plane floated above, he felt the murmur of it droning within him, bringing to light an ancient, long forgotten feeling. He followed the sound floating left to right, followed it as it crossed the avenues and bounced off the sides of cars and old looking buildings, as if bringing joy to everything it touched: the tobacco store; the bookstore; and his favorite hobby shop. His instincts were verified as the plane emerged from beneath the overcast like an apparition. Slowly at first, winking out of the gray, then back in, clouds tumbled beneath her engines in sporadic bursts of chowdery wisps giving way to the greasy belly of the Boeing 737 airliner as it descended ever slowly toward the Burlington airport beyond the horizon. It will land, he thought, at a hallowed field of cinderblock and smooth concrete, with its tall, brick control tower waiting, like an impatient, loyal, golden retriever. Then it disappeared toward the distant north.

The telephone rang.

"Mrs. Sullivan?"

"Yes," Margaret said.

"I...I don't know if you remember me. I'm Everet Strong, Ely's...um...father."

She had to sit down. Once again she felt like the wind had been knocked out of her chest. She cleared her throat.

"Yes, I do remember you."

"I am so sorry about Sandy. There hasn't been a day that has gone by—"

"Yes, we all feel that way," she interrupted.

"I just want you to know that I am here. My plane just arrived and I am going to be ready to meet you and Ellison wherever you, or he, choose."

She cursed Mike, wondering how Trish could have married such a louse. "Didn't Mike tell you that Ely doesn't want to meet you?"

He paused. "No. He didn't."

"I'm sorry, Everet, but a meeting is impossible. Ely told me that he doesn't want to. I can't force him, you know, especially now...and Mike was supposed to call you back and..."

"Margaret, I'm here. I came all the way from Pennsylvania. I can't tell you how intense my feelings were when I heard. I went from such great sadness at hearing of Sandy's death, then to such joy—such elation—when I heard about Ely. I just have to see him. There is so much I want to learn about him: what he looks like; what his hobbies are; how he was raised...Christ, everything—he's my own flesh and blood! Please, Margaret, just let us meet once, somewhere," Everet pleaded.

She felt sorry for him. He sounded desperate. Maybe...maybe meeting him wasn't such a bad thing...maybe it was exactly what Ely needed. He had been so down lately.

"Listen, Everet," she coughed, "I can tell that you only mean well for the boy, and maybe you're exactly what he needs in his life right now. I know he told me he just wanted to be left alone. But maybe it would be okay..." she hesitated, "maybe I can bring him to you after school."

"Thank you, Margaret."

"I'll try and bring him to the cemetery on Allen Street in town, Sandy's grave, four o'clock. Do you think you can find it?"

"Is there more than one cemetery on Allen Street?"

"That's the only one, and her grave is the only new looking one. I make no promises though, if he doesn't want to go I can't force him."

"I understand," Everet said. "I'll be there."

"No promises."

"No promises."

She hung up.

When the bell rang ending his school day, he was in no particular hurry to go home. It felt good to be out among the living. He carefully closed his textbook and placed it into his backpack, and took out the most current copy of Airways magazine, unfolded it, and began to admire the pictures of brightly painted airliners as he pulled the straps over his shoulders. He read as he walked, looking only peripherally at sidewalk cracks and stopping for traffic at the busy intersection near the center of town. The sun broke through the afternoon clouds, and he followed his shadow as he walked. He did not notice the red rental car drive slowly past, headed toward the edge of town. He crossed the street, looking up only for a moment as a sport utility vehicle honked as it swerved and stopped. He folded his magazine, shoved it into his back pocket and entered the hobby shop across from the park.

Margaret sat with her coat fully buttoned and waited on the couch across from the regulator clock. The four loud chimes startled her as she lowered her woman's magazine and checked the time on the clock against the time on her watch. Her watch was fast. She pulled the crown and reset it to the time on the wall clock and clicked it back in. Ely was not usually this late, she thought. She looked at the clock at five past, then again at ten past. She kept raising and lowering her magazine until she could no longer concentrate on the article. It was driving her crazy continuously checking the clock. While she forced herself to read, she knew that more than the clock distracted her from comprehending what she read. She couldn't help but think about what was best for Ellison. The thought of Everet in his life made sense now more than ever. Whoever he was, this man from Pennsylvania who apparently moved around a lot, sounded nice. At least he had some sort of job. If it turned out that he was a decent man, then of course he would be a good influence on his son's life. Ellison needed someone exactly like that. She began to panic. Where was Ely?

Sandy's resting place was vivid in the winter sun. The cemetery was on a rolling hillside with expertly placed hardwoods plunging toward the sky between even rows of monuments. Everet caught a whiff of wet oak leaves as a squirrel dashed between a nut stash and a nearby tree trunk repeatedly. His watch read 4:40. The town just wasn't that big. It wouldn't take more than five minutes to get from anywhere in town to the cemetery. It was obvious that Ely wasn't coming. He didn't blame him. Thoughts of meeting his son drifted slowly into the realm of impossibility.

"No promises," he mumbled.

He said his good-byes to Sandy as he knelt over the muddy spot in the grass that was her grave. He'd thought he might one day see her again, but not like this. Knowing that she was dead brought back memories of her attractiveness in college, her brash demeanor that he found so beguiling then, and their remarkable meeting a few years later, the one that produced Ely. Knowing he existed also meant that a part of Sandy was still alive, somewhere.

His body filled with anxiety knowing that their meeting time had long passed and still there was no sign of Ely. He paced. He tried to put himself in Ely's position, a boy having recently lost his mother now finding out that his real father is alive, and well, and wanting to see him. How must that feel? Would he want to see his father after fifteen years? It would depend. Why hadn't Ely met his father until now? Why mess up a perfectly good life with a whole new set of grown up baggage? Maybe he didn't realize that neither had known of the other. Maybe Ely thought his real father was just a deadbeat. No, it was selfish of him to expect Ely to want to know him after so long.

At least he got to be there, to say his good-byes to a woman he had once loved, and put her into his past once again. At least he had a chance, he thought, shoving his hands into his pockets, to meet Ely. He slowly walked toward his rental car, a defeated man.

Ely read as he walked home from the hobby store...

The door swung open.

"Where were you?" Margaret asked.

"At the hobby shop," Ely said.

"Drop your things, I have somewhere to take you."

"Where?"

"Don't ask. Let's just go and get this over with," she said.

"Oh, no."

"Hurry!"

"No, this can't be happening…"

She mustered up all the energy that she could, pulling on the boy with the strength she had twenty years earlier, drawing and leaning on him as she walked.

"Get in!" she demanded with a quivering voice. She grabbed on to the car as she walked around to the other side, pulled open the door and dropped herself into the driver's seat. With a shaking hand, she placed the key into the ignition and started the car. A car skidded to a stop behind her as she backed into traffic without looking, then she jammed the accelerator, squealing her own tires, speeding off toward the cemetery.

"Grandma, why are you driving so fast?" Ely said.

"We're late. He might not even be there anymore."

She slowed to a jogger's pace through a four-way intersection, turned the corner on Allen Street, and drove over the curb into the cemetery.

"There," she coughed, out of breath, "that fellow by the red car. I think that's him."

"I still don't feel comfortable about this."

She slowed to a stop behind the red car, jerked the transmission lever into *Park*, and turned toward Ely.

"At first I was against you knowing who your real father was. Once the word got out, it was too late. Now my mind has totally changed. You need someone in your life to talk to besides your Uncle Mike. Besides…a decrepit old lady"

"I…I…I…I don't know…" he said.

"You're nervous. That's to be expected. Go out and meet him at least. He came all the way from Pennsylvania."

"No, I…I can't!" he said.

"You have to." She began coughing and patting herself on the chest, "If you don't do it, you may regret it the rest of your life," she said.

"But, Grandma…"

"Do it!"

Everet had his hand on the door handle of the red rental car. He was about to open it when the sight of another car rambling up the cemetery drive made his heart beat faster.

"Ely!"

He released the handle and stood statue-like as the car stopped short just in front of him. He had difficulty keeping the grin from his face as he saw the two through their windshield. Slowly, the passenger side door opened and out came a tall, young man wearing an unzipped winter coat, white tennis shoes and baggy jeans. His hair was dark like his own, but his eyes were all Sandy's. Seeing him was like seeing a part of Sandy all over again, and a part of him had been sent back in time.

Ely felt weird seeing his father for the first time; he couldn't think of anything to say.

"Hello, Ellison. I'm your dad. My name is...Everet. Everet Strong." Holding out his hand seemed the right thing to do, though it was uncomfortable for him too.

Ely slowly reached toward his hand.

"Hello," he replied.

They stared at each other for a moment. Neither knew where to begin.

"I am so sorry about you mother."

Ely said nothing, but kicked a small pebble by his foot.

"She was very special. Very special," he said, and then cleared his throat sensing Ely's distrust. "Of course you know that."

Ely's eyes squinted in the sun as he looked at his father, and then he turned away.

Everet motioned toward Margaret that he would like to walk along the road with the boy. She nodded her head.

"Ely, I don't know what you know. Maybe we both only know one side of the story," Everet said.

"All I know is that my life has been pretty shitty lately. Honestly, learning about you hasn't helped. I haven't heard from my father, Jake, since he left, which was bad enough. Learning that I had another father, a real father, and not hearing from him either, is just about as bad as it gets. What the hell did I do to deserve that?"

"Nothing. You did nothing."

The two walked some more, turning onto the sod toward Sandy's grave, and avoiding the patches of melting snow.

"Ely, I never even knew you existed. Sandy…your mom, never told me. If I had known about you, life would have been very different for the both of us, I promise you. When I heard last week that I had another son, I was overjoyed."

"You never knew?" Ely turned toward him.

"No. I never even knew you existed."

"Then how?" Ely asked.

"We have all the time in the world to talk about it. Someday I will tell you all about us, your mother and me. She was so special. I loved her so, back then."

They came to a stop at Sandy's grave.

"They did a nice job picking out this place," Everet said, pulling an index finger along the corner of his right eye.

"She mentioned once to my grandmother that this place seemed like a little corner of heaven on earth."

"It is, I must say."

Everet raised his hand and wiped wetness from the corner of his other eye. As he did, Ely saw the reflection from his unusual watch. Ely couldn't keep his eyes from it, and Everet noticed.

He unbuckled it from his wrist and handed it to him.

Take it," Everet said.

Ely studied it in the sunlight. "It's a pilot watch," he said.

"Yeah," he replied, "they make us wear those. You can have that."

"You're a pilot?"

"Well, yes. And I, or, your mother and I, met in an aviation class a long time ago. She sure had a knack for it. I wish she'd continued. Anyway, I've been one for seventeen years."

"Seventeen years?"

"You like planes, Ely?"

"Do I?" Ely viewed his father differently. Was this where he got it from, this obsession, this love, this desire? Having two parents who flew made sense now. "There is nothing I'd rather do than fly," he said.

"Me, too."

Ely carefully pulled the Airways magazine from his back pocket and unfolded it. "See?"

"I'll be damned," Everet said, stunned.

"And inside...this guy, I love this guy." Ely paged through the magazine and stopped on a story by Chet Jetzen, pointing to his picture. "He's my fav—Hey..."

"You know, Ely..."

"This picture of Chet at the top of the column...He looks...He looks like you!"

"Son," he hesitated...

"...that's my pen name."

PART III

POST TRAGEDY

Since September, the Journal

San Francisco, at the hotel, room # 3108. These times I cherish greatly. My attitude is great. The weather was good all the way from New York City. It is because I finally feel confident and a little seasoned in the airplane, and can relax and converse freely with my captain. My good attitude brings forth his, I think, which only makes life more enjoyable. I am still thinking about how much fun "Cookie Girl" and I had in Portland, ME, and how well it all went. The sun shines here in San Francisco this morning. I had breakfast and coffee early at the coffee house next door. People are kitschy here.

After landing the airplane yesterday afternoon and checking into the hotel, the crew went their separate ways, which was a nice change. I walked over Nob Hill to Fisherman's Wharf, then Pier 39, and found a place that rents yachts as hotel rooms (making a mental note for a future stay with Cookie), and ate Chinese. I later happened upon a crew of a fishing boat who offered to take me on a tour of the bay, which was nice. Cookie will meet me at the gate tonight when we return.

[09-11-01]

As the chaos unfolds in New York and Washington D.C., my phone rings. Mom is the first to call. She wants to know that I wasn't one of the unfortunate pilots who were hijacked, their planes turned into missiles. I watch as it happens live on television. The massive World Trade Center collapses, first one tower, then the next in giant plumes of debris. Casualties must number in the thousands, perhaps a million, I don't know. This is not the time to be trigger-happy. Americans will want vengeance, and they will want blood. To deploy nuclear weapons would mean suicide. It is surreal. I have flown by the towers on numerous occasions. They defined the New York City skyline—tall, shiny. Nothing is sacred. I cannot watch. I must do what I had originally planned. To relieve my mind, I will paint my deck.

[09-12-01]

The fallout continues. No more planes crash into buildings. There is digging in mountains of remnants of the two one-time tallest buildings in the world. Three hundred firefighters lost—many policemen. I painted my deck with Cookie's help, and it took the rest of the day. I had to occupy my mind, to reflect on the possibility of my own demise, or my friend's, should it have been us. A chilling thought. I am still in shock after seeing my brothers and their machines flown full throttle into the side of buildings. No airplanes flew yesterday or today. The sky is without contrails, without sound. It is the first time since the first plane flew that no civilian planes fly. I should be on a trip today, but instead closely monitor my schedule via computer. Everything is cancelled.

At least I am home. Some of my friends are stuck in hotels throughout the world. Other friends in Texas have gathered to hold a drunken vigil tonight. I am lucky, I guess.

[09-13-10]

As I go through my lot in life, to fly passenger jets for a living, I learn over and over that it is a continual test of courage. A pilot faces fear often, be it bad weather, mechanical problem, or maniacal. And I have wondered what it is like living life without certain fear. Total contentedness, or complacency, is unfamiliar to pilots for good reason. To be unafraid is to be unaware. Brave men are most fearful, but they continue anyway, which is why they are brave. A firefighter comes to mind.

I am supposed to fly to Boston tomorrow, but I don't think it will happen. More pilot imposters have been caught in New York despite increased security. Have any slipped through? In my mind, I prepare to kill any man who strikes at me while I am at the controls. And, when it isn't my turn to fly, I will focus on the cockpit door, crash axe in hand, knife blade in the other, and be ready to kill. Is this civility? Where has peace and trust gone? Tonight it rains.

[09-14-01]

This morning, as I lie in bed and listen, I hear no planes. Still. I am checking my airline's web site to see if I am flying this afternoon.

There is a certain "anointing" taking place at the national cathedral now. There is patriotism and a religious "knighting" of ourselves, getting "God" on our side. We don't see it that way of course, we see it as paying homage to those who gave their lives in the tragedy. But, we are anointing ourselves right now, to fix those who dealt with us so heinously—mentally, and emotionally—and we are on the side of "right" as, unfortunately, our enemies also believe. Thought and logic will not cause self-destruction, but mankind's interpretation of what "God" is may.

[09-15-01]

Pete called this morning to say that he heard that our airline would be downsizing by 20 percent and furloughing 12,000 (total) employees. Are we rumor whores? Am I getting nervous about things that may not affect me at all?

[09-17-01]

I ran the numbers. It looks as though I will continue to work even after the furloughs, but I no longer can hold my captain bid, another good reason to avoid debt. Our stock is down to $20. It's been around $60. It has to be unrealistically low. The call to furlough may have backfired. I certainly hope so.

[09-19-01]

New York. Today I flew for the first time since the attack. I was nervous, suffering from a cold, as maybe others had. I wouldn't dare call in sick though; we all have to continue to work. We have to continue to buy tickets, to travel, to play.

The air is a brown haze. There is a gaping hole where spires used to be. I feel like I am looking at a friend who is missing an arm and it just doesn't look natural. The air is scented with an unfamiliar odor of what I can best describe as burned rubber, and molten metal, and perhaps...charred flesh. I first noticed this stench descending through 9,000 feet just crossing over the Pennsylvania border.

The stock market dropped over 10 percent in a single day, airlines are furloughing and begging for assistance from the government or else potentially filing for bankruptcy in a few months. It all seems so precarious. We are our own worst enemy. We need a leader to instill confidence in the people, to show that we succeed or fail by our own design. Are we all weak? Do we wither when a single bully acts or do we fight?

[09-26-01]

New York again. Mom's birthday. There is something comforting about the sound of airplanes as they roar every few seconds just beyond my hotel window. I will sleep, but lightly tonight.

[10-03-01]

Mexico. It rains under a thick overcast. The view from my hotel reminds me of the Pacific: block buildings; graffiti; wild drivers; and a foreign smell in the air. It is about 65 degrees here, which seems strange for south of the border. Unexplainable things occur, as seems to be the case on the last day of a four-day trip. The captain and I briefed all that we could on the way down. We were vigilant, especially since we were both new to the area. In the soup, there was a last minute runway change, a new approach and then my Symbol Generator failed causing me to lose most of my navigational instruments. I regained them a short time later. The controller kept us unusually high, even for the terrain, and then cleared us for the approach. We came down like a rock and broke out at 500'. It's hard not to get frazzled.

[11-30-01]

Las Vegas, NV. Sometimes they pick us up in long, stretch limousines when they are available. Sometimes, like when business travel is way down, we get luxury hotel rooms like the one I am staying in. This is a two-floor suite with a bedroom loft upstairs, Jacuzzi on the stairway landing, fireplace by the bed. I'm writing at the marble bar. It's not usually like this. This must be part of the business and vacationer fallout after September 11.

I lost another $60 on this overnight. Looks like another Subway sandwich for dinner.

[12-31-01]

Florida. I had lunch facing the marina waterway at the hotel. Boats trolled past as it gently rained from slate clouds. Some were very large and I wondered who had the money for such extravagances. Most of the owners, I assumed, were overextended financially, or there are many more wealthy people in this world than I am aware of. Still, it was relaxing to eat my turkey sandwich at the window, gazing at them.

The young couple sitting near me appears to be newlyweds. The husband talked endlessly about the boats and their peculiarities, not unlike the way pilots speak of airplanes. The girl's eyes glazed over as she sat quietly listening.

[01-16-02]

I have been flying a lot of red-eye flights this month, which has allowed me to spend more time at home doing fixer-up projects. After painting the bathroom, I drilled into the wall to hang the towel rack. I hit an electrical supply cord on the other side, zapping my drill. Then I had to cut into the wall to fix it.

[05-15-02]

New York City. It was windy last night. We held over Philly after cruising low and using precious fuel. LaGuardia is a bastard of an airport, designed for use during an earlier time like much of New York. Now, it is undersized, and over utilized, and flying into it is like the car traffic around the airport, tight corridors filled with too many planes making tight turns in windy conditions. Though rules abound in every aspect of New York, from "No Parking," to "No U-turn," only those who break them seem to get anything done. It is no wonder that the Mob flourished here, because it seems that those who abide by rules get left behind, and with few exceptions flying is the same here. "The squeaky wheel gets the grease," (no matter how many times ground control tells you not to call), and, "The early bird gets the worm."

My captain is young and competent. He has taken the place of a nervous man who took the place of another nervous man. I find that those who enjoy the job do so because they are friendly and personable, and they see mirrors in us all. Being nervous is common among line pilots. I wonder if it is the same in all walks of life or if it is prevalent because being a captain of a sizable vessel causes one to view life differently. Certainly, a captain gets more respect from people, but there is no greater responsibility and concern for real world life and death issues than he has.

[05-24-02]

Louisiana. Sometimes having an adventure gets our mind on other things. The cab was late in picking us up to go to the restaurant. It turned out to be a rickety thing, and though the driver seemed harmless, he stopped to pick up a scary looking buddy. For a while, I thought we might get shanghaied in the back of that rickety old cab. We found the place safely, which turned out in all its splendor to be a dive, but the food was good, as it often is in such places—catfish, crawfish, alligator and frogs legs. And we talked some. I laughed initially when my captain told me that we should have dropped a nuclear bomb on Kabul, but then I saw that he was serious.

[05-29-02]

This morning, on rotation, we hit a seagull just above my windshield. It sounded like a baseball bat smacking the window, and I flinched.

[06-08-02]

I think it is the ultimate goal for a person to work a part time job and have a full time income. Some people can do it. Some say that is what I do, particularly when I drop a trip once in a while and maximize vacation. Sometimes we pilots get agitated when we only get fourteen days off a month. But, though it sounds like a lot of time at home, it really doesn't relate that we are actually gone a lot. We spend four days away at a time and, as was the case last month, fifteen nights a month in a hotel room. I have gone through spurts of not sleeping well because of the different beds, and different wake-up times each day. One night in New York, I get to the hotel after midnight and a few days later my alarm clock wakes me at 4:15 AM, a cycle that will continue throughout my career. So it is no wonder why many of us walk through the terminal with bags under our eyes.

[08-12-02]

California. Sometimes I feel like I have a surreal job. Though it's hard to explain, it is sometimes like throwing your body off a cliff, because someone said the water was probably deep enough for a soft landing. Air travel is extremely safe, but nothing is absolute. Today we received a plane in New York, her rudder written up by the previous crew with a vibration. A rudder vibration is no joke in a 737 and I was pleased to see maintenance hard at work trying to locate the problem. But they found nothing out of the ordinary. Following proper procedure, they asked us if we would take the plane and make note of any vibrations in the rudder once we were airborne. The captain and I discussed the situation in depth and concluded that as long as everything checked out from a maintenance standpoint, we would accept the plane. It became what we call "an acceptable risk."

Passengers are usually unaware of these "acceptable risks," some people may say there was no risk at all as long as everything checked out. But an airplane is a machine, guided by, designed by, and fixed by humans. And an "acceptable risk" is like taking a plunge off a cliff when the water depth is not precisely known.

This is just a glimpse into an airline pilot's life post September 11th. In looking back on the year, the one thing that is apparent is that the first entry, prior to the 11th, was almost blissfully content. What follows, takes on almost a nightmarish tone, a slogging through life until the initial shock, and preparation for personal repercussions subsides. Though I tried in vain to continue as I had before, denying that the world really had changed, I have come to the realization that the industry at least, may never be as it was before. That long lines at security, having to endure degrading fondling by security officials, and higher ticket prices are here to stay. And the result of these undesirable experiences is fewer passengers, smaller planes, and fewer jobs.

But what I have also gleaned from revisiting this post September 11th year, and something I can always be pleased about, is that there is still no other profession I would rather be in. It is interesting, and challenging, and worthwhile, and should the budgetary guillotine fall on me, as it has for many of my comrades in the industry, I'll find a way to get by, and get back to the cockpit.

The Aviator behind the Façade

I thumb through the myriad of switches during the *receiving aircraft* flow. One by one, a bell sounds, the control wheel shakes, then an electronic voice yells "pull-up," and I tap the FMC computer by my left knee with index and middle finger alternately, programming it with the prepared flight plan in my other hand. My fingers move fast, and though I always do my receiving check the same way every time, I inadvertently leave a switch unswitched or a pump unpumping which keeps me adequately paranoid. The checklist confirms my healthy paranoia.

It was not long ago when I first upgraded to the copilot's seat of the 737 that there was so much to do I was barely able to catch up before we were cleared into position on the runway, and often sweat dripped down my cheeks so much that the captain, who felt sorry for me, would stop the plane and wait until I caught up. He saw something worth being patient for and I am the product of many patient and understanding captains like him.

Thankfully now, I am able to sit at ease and ponder the course of our trip before the cabin door is closed, having completed the required checks at a more experienced, efficient speed. This captain, Lou, a man I have flown with before, is equally at ease knowing that his copilot isn't stuck in row 20 from the get go, so we can concentrate on other things, generally parts of the female anatomy, or a new card trick he has learned, or if I am lucky, he would pat the Hohner Blues Harmonica in his shirt pocket and nod as though he had the answer to any question right there. To speak of numbers, and limits, and procedures became tedious for most of us a month or two after flying the line as we became intimately familiar with the running of the ship. Of course, there are plenty of examples of this regurgitation of minutia at various levels. There is the captain whose "Ops" manual is pulled out for every minuscule decision, and though it may be an edition only a few months old, its corners are browned and dog-eared as though it spent a lifetime being carried in young Abe Lincoln's back pocket as he walked to school. And it is particularly disheartening to realize you are flying with this sort of bookish commander at the beginning of a long four day trip, as the odds of conversing about anything more risqué than the domestic duty time limits are slim to none.

Equally disheartening, given how easy flying an airliner can be, and a reason to focus on minutia, is to find one's self sitting next to the micro manager who nearly bursts a temple vessel when a ramp serviceman forgets a wand, or the cabin door is closed a few minutes late, or his coffee isn't beige enough, or the signature on the fuel slip is indecipherable. The list is endless, yet true. So it is with utmost pleasure I am flying with Lou this evening.

His face is chubby, made so by years of smiling at his own jokes while eating untold crew meals served affectionately to him by adoring flight attendants. They come up with any reason to dawdle on the flight deck to be with him, to swim in his entertainment of magic tricks, singing and jokes told with timing every bit as good as Rodney Dangerfield's. I eat well when I am with Lou, since they treat any lucky sidekick of his as though he was in the inner circle. This might explain why the *Op's Commander*, and *Temple Blower* are much thinner than Lou, by the way.

The New Generation 737 jiggles with a trickling of passengers. The smell of freshly brewed coffee mixes with a recent spray of aromatic pillows of perfume from the first class flight attendant. I can hear her voice descending from the mumble of greetings and questions of business-suited men with boarding passes clenched in tired fists. Her voice is angelic and I can sense that Lou is as sweet on her as I am, but she wears a blinding diamond on her left hand, which we noticed immediately, undoubtedly given to her by an intelligent man who knows the value of his catch, and whom we both despise. In the midst of the controlled chaos of boarding, she finds the time to take our requests for beverages before the cockpit door is closed. Without hesitation, Lou orders his usual mug of coffee—regular style. I follow suit identically, because to have my drink as Lou does somehow makes it taste all the more interesting, and in less than a minute our mugs arrive and our angel is awash in the gratitude of two overly thankful men, and I can feel the tingle of her blush in the balls of my feet. He slurps his coffee and exhales. Only then was he fully prepared to enjoy our trek to its maximum effect and I knew exactly how he felt once I did the same.

We push in the usual way. The cockpit door is locked and we begin not an evening of work, but a psychological dissection of each other in a way that only people strapped next to each other for many hours inevitably do. And trust among flight crews is preponderate. Without it, we cannot survive the judgment of our partner, we cannot survive a challenging landing by him; we may not survive an FAA inquiry; we may not survive anything at all. It is therefore inevitable that we delve into the deepest, darkest, recesses of our very being as quickly as possible, which is, of course, solely in the interest of safety. It is not done with scalpels or knives, but rather with narrow and seemingly benign questions and comments, as jumping off points that open crevasses of attitudes, strengths, weaknesses and blind-spots, hidden behind the unflappable façade that we each project.

I remember how nice it felt, when I was a captain on smaller commuter planes, to taxi the plane on the tarmac of a busy, international airport. Nothing pumps the ego like being in command of a very expensive vessel and Lou knows this. More is learned about a copilot than what is spoken: the yearning look in one's eyes toward the throttles; the jacking of the seat for the better view; the unabashed sigh once all the paperwork is done; the envy.

"Take her, I've got to get something out of my flight bag," he says. And without a word, my fingertips slip onto the vibrating throttles of the rolling monolith and I inch them toward 30 percent. My toes touch the pedals, turning the nose wheel in limited capacity, just enough to keep the yellow centerline below my crotch. I glance at him and his head is down in such a way that he couldn't possibly see where we are going, and I am without question, totally in control. I can feel the power of command as I once had before and the feeling of it pumps through my veins like an elixir.

I make our call to ground and receive clearance to taxi to the runway, giving way to a Southwest 737 approaching from our left to right. As he rolls by, I can make out the faces of the pilots sitting in the pointy section of their bird and can't help but wonder if they are interacting as delightfully as Lou and I, or if one of them is a Temple Blower. Lou finds his US HI map, refolding it to reveal our course, and then places it on the clipboard by his side. Having a real, old fashioned, paper map handy is an easy habit to get out of when you have a glass cockpit with a moving map display, but more than once I have been rerouted and even lost my Flight Management Computer, causing me considerable wonder at where we actually were at the time. He's prepared, I see, and I trust him as he does me.

"You're doing such a nice job you can take it all the way to the runway if you want," he says. I flash a smile, and ease her to a stop just behind Southwest's tarnished exhaust. Once cleared for take off, they eat most of the runway, obviously heavily laden with fuel, as their fuselage inches upward, Phoenix bound. Lou drives us onto the runway after they depart. His tiller wheel has more authority over my foot pedals and can make the 90-degree turn onto the numbers much better than I can.

"You have the jet," he says, and once again relinquishes the throttles over to me. To hear another say, "You have the jet," is the realization of a thousand nights of dreaming for the airplane-obsessed teenager, and I never forgot how I longed to find myself here. It is no accident that Lou repeated the words that bring forth an unimaginable feeling of accomplishment as I am sure that he, too, a military and airline flyer for over thirty years, feels the honey of it float within his brain.

The moment the throttles of an airliner move, life takes on an entirely new meaning. We are no longer just ordinary human beings, but men who accept the task of safely moving a hundred people skyward in a machine, which is statistically destined to fail in some form one day. As our speed increases, we feel every flaw in the runway with increasing rapidity. The act of multiple scenarios ranging from a rejected take off, to continuing with a flaming engine, to a bird strike, run through my mind, with equally increasing rapidity. There is a similar paranoia felt by a wealthy man walking down a dark city alley late at night knowing a mugger is out there...somewhere. Only when the thumping wheels leave the runway and a sufficient amount of altitude is below my body, does the feeling of Jack the Ripper lurking in the shadows subside.

We are switched over to subsequent controllers about every minute and Lou checks on with his best pilot radio voice—deeper, serious, and authoritative. He holds the hand mike sideways in his left hand, pressing the transmit button, not with the tip of his index finger, but by the base, just above the knuckle, in a way he has grown accustomed to over the decades, in a way that becomes a captain. He dangles it on the side window egress handle between replies, and pulls it infectiously close to his lips as he speaks. It smells of coffee.

The very first time you fly with a captain there is a mental *feeling-out*, not dissimilar to the examination between two lone wolves, meeting each other without their respective packs. Wariness prevails until you are proven safe and trustworthy. One can only hope to fly through a hurricane immediately after being introduced to gain immediate trust and respect rather than build it over the course of a three-day trip in weather so nice that anyone can look good. Luckily, I passed muster with Lou sometime not too far into our first day together before the harmonica came out.

The dreary evening grayness died with a burst of salmon orange, and our climbing turn was fantastically evident once above the clouds. The sun sunk below the horizon and the orange faded to red, to royal blue, then to black as stars twinkled high above Indiana. Once above the clouds, the ride smoothed out. Lou pointed to me with his index finger, then made the "1" signal informing me that I was to handle the number one radio while he made the seat belt P.A. to the passengers. Upon completion of his arrival time and seat belt announcement, not a second after replacing the mike, Angel knocked her secret knock upon the cockpit door and I tapped the door unlock button.

"Hot towels?" she asked, tonging one in Lou's direction.

"Why, but of course, my dear, how could I resist such a sweet offer? Did you happen to catch my informative chat?" he said in his best British dialect.

She tonged another in my direction. "You know, when you lie about us being the three most highly awarded Flight Attendants in the industry they expect us to live up to that," she said.

"Lie? Whatsoever do you mean?"

Angel smirked and rolled her eyes. She disappeared and returned a moment later with two mugs of Java and a basket of rolls.

"This will tide you over until my service is complete."

"Thank you, sweetheart," I said. Lou bit into a roll and winked as she left.

To the novice pilot, the speed at which the air traffic controller speaks is overwhelming when in the context of a busy major airport. To the untrained ear, it sounds literally as if they speak a foreign language consisting mostly of numbers, but it doesn't take long to realize that what they say consists of only a few phrases, changing the airplane's call sign between commands. Inevitably, one learns to listen to what is happening while carrying on a separate conversation with your partner while understanding both at the same time, sort of the way a fly's eyeball works, only it sees about a thousand images at once and still bumps into walls. That's not to say that one or two calls are not occasionally missed, but that likely occurs more frequently with Ops Commander types who converse more intensely, but with less enjoyment on my part.

For the next hour, I am feeling as though I am sitting next to an old friend at a bar. Our topics of conversation range from the health of our mothers, to favorite fishing spots, to which of our current flight attendants had the highest degree of muliebrity and hypothetically, who of us had the better chance of ever finding out. Lou cracks another joke, his twelfth this evening, and I laugh as a good friend would whether they were funny or not. This one was funny.

By now, the night is in full bloom and, once past Michigan, we leave the undercast behind. Chicago unfurls below us, its twinkling lights blanketing the cityscape, and they become our topic of debate—phosphorous or tungsten. Phosphorous, we conclude, millions of phosphorous lights. The penetrating blackness of Lake Michigan contrasts the brightness of the Magnificent Mile and the fingers of golden highways spread endlessly to the suburbs. The cockpit lights are dimmed except for the most important instruments making the display below even more extraordinary, giving us the illusion of hovering.

I pick up the interphone and ring the back. Margaret, our second flight attendant, picks up. "Come up," I say, "it's beautiful out here." She hangs up. Moments later, she knocks her secret knock on the cockpit door and, upon entering, steps up to the center console. Angel and our third flight attendant, Tibby, follow her. There are five of us in this tiny compartment in the dark, saying not a word, but absorbing the vast beauty of Chicago from the air. Lou and I have Chicago Center clucking away in our earpieces, which, only to a pilot, add to the splendor, but to the girls we are phantoms floating peacefully in the night. The three sets of perfumes combined have the bouquet of an old fish bowl and I am mildly taken aback, and the lusciousness of their company is short lived as we hear someone chiming for a fresh drink in the back. One by one they depart, Margaret being the slowest to leave, her hand had been on Lou's shoulder the entire time.

"She wants you," I say.

He glances at the progress page on the FMC, noting our arrival time. "You think so?"

It occurs to me that Lou doesn't have a wedding ring on and Margaret is a very nice looking woman close to Lou's age.

"Yeah, you could do well to have her, being the old spinster you are and all," I say jokingly.

In a rare break of chatter from Chicago Center, I hear him sigh deeply, close-mouthed. His eyes fix on infinity beyond his window.

"I'm married."

"You? I didn't know. Do you have a picture of her?" I am curious to see what kind of patient woman would be married to him.

Without taking his eyes from whatever it was he looked at, he, in an unusually sober mood, reaches into his aft right coat pocket and pulls out his wallet. With his left hand, he turns on the light above the center console and then thumbs through the small, clear pages containing credit cards and his driver's license. He pulls out a well-worn picture of his family: his wife and a young girl to his left. I gather from the blackness of his hair that the picture was at least ten years old.

"There she is; that's my wife."

Her features are sharp and lean—I expected more of a grandmotherly type—but she is very pretty and I, being single, envied him.

"She's very beautiful. And that's your daughter?"

I wait.

I repeated, "That's your dau…"

"Was."

I am confused.

"Was my daughter," he says. "She died at thirteen."

His voice quivers as he relates the events that lead to her death…the day they found out, the months of painful cancer treatment, the day he kissed her cold, blue lips good-bye. His wife has been an alcoholic recluse for the five years since.

There is nothing I can say. I thought I could relate to anything, any problem, any situation, but I am speechless.

I don't see him wipe the corners of his eyes.

He requests "Direct Palmdale" from Chicago Center.

"Expect that from Minneapolis," the controller replies and switches us over.

With the lights of Chicago a distant memory, and the Iowa farmland our new diversion, he plays a child's lullaby softly on his harmonica. And I bank gently toward California.

Orange Colored Sky

Olive pulls at the collar of her blouse. Although the temperature inside New York's Kennedy Airport terminal is a constant 70 degrees, it seems uncomfortably cold to her. She buttons the top button on her neck, which makes her black skirt and white blouse look like more suitable attire for a schoolteacher or an Amish girl instead of a homemaker and mother of five. It is not uncommon for her to be in a melancholy mood either; after all, she is sixty-three years old, her children are grown, the house is usually empty, and life has not been always easy. But Harold made it easy...most of the time.

She takes a seat at the departure gate facing the food court and gazes into the airport activity. The Middle East explodes again, and again, as told to her on the airport television, which cycles through its programming every twenty minutes. Noise is continuous—people are paged over the public address system periodically, and flights are called with accents so thick that she can't decipher them, but she knows when her flight will leave, exactly five o'clock, and she knows Harold will also be there, which is why she stops worrying.

A man pushes a jingling cart filled with open liquor bottles slowly down the concourse. Another man pulls a roll-aboard suitcase with an oblong wheel and it clicks like a continuous little machine gun at his heels. A maintenance man with a fast food bag turns down the volume of his portable radio; a ramp man with an orange vest, like the kind worn by hunters, talks on a cell phone. A petite woman laughs as a dog yaps, and a young boy holds his mother's hand. Another man pushes a cart with beer kegs. She notices this parade of humanity, realizing for the first time that she is as they are, just people—as insignificant as ants on a sidewalk.

Five short nuns in blue and gray habits contemplate a hamburger as a male flight attendant passes them with a wink and smile. A drug abuse message plays on the unwatched television that hangs from the ceiling while a confused looking old man in a blue denim shirt walks by. A woman takes a newspaper left on a chair by a departed passenger, and looks as though she found a million dollars. A young man with an annoyed expression talks distractedly on a cell phone, his eyes follow the paths cut by an occasional young woman passing by. Judging by the wrinkles on his forehead, he appears to be talking with his girlfriend. An old man with a scowl on his face reads a men's magazine that, thankfully, Harold would never read.

Employees wearing absurdly baggy clothes leave the fast food restaurant after their shift. A heavy woman puffs by in blue sandals that slide across the floor with a *ka-thwap* sound, grasping at her purse. More people tote backpacks than carry suitcases.

A gentle breeze presses against Olive's hair from an overhead duct. It smells faintly of cooked hotdogs, and sweet, Chinese noodles. A woman talks loudly over the intercom announcing the boarding of another flight, and Olive wonders if she is aware that her harried voice is amplified. People wear mostly black; there is no floral, pastel, or paisley, as the general mood of New York is black these days, and she contemplates her own clothes for a moment. People look away as her eyes meet theirs. Most are generally subdued, sitting quietly in the solace of their own thoughts among hundreds of others in blue vinyl seats surrounding her. The president makes a speech that is heeded by a single janitor. An old lady is hunched; osteoporosis bending her white haired head, as she defiantly walks by a man pushing an empty wheelchair.

There are chubby girls in belly shirts, skinny girls in belly shirts, all speaking on cell phones. People from all corners of the globe converge in the food court waiting for their flights. A hum becomes louder and an electric cart carrying a mother and father and two obese children rolls slowly by. The driver excuses herself loudly every ten seconds. Seemingly embarrassed and annoyed, people move to the side reluctantly. Olive thought she saw a sign on the side that reads: "Only for use by people with disabilities." The sun shines directly onto the terrazzo floor through windows along the ceiling and she wonders how such a beautiful floor came to be.

Suddenly, Olive becomes aware of a man singing *Orange Colored Sky*[1], from the speakers hidden in the ceiling. She hears it faintly at first, then, though there is activity all around her, it is all she can hear. Nat King Cole sings with the classical, buttery, smoothness that evokes an earlier era, and the quality of the recording sounds just as pristine:

> *"I was walking along,*
> *Minding my business,*
> *When out from an orange-colored sky...*
> *Flash!*
> *Bam!*
> *Alakazam!*
> *Wonderful you came by..."*

And she is immersed in the memory it conjures.

That was our song, she thinks. So long ago, she had forgotten. Harold would sing it sometimes just to embarrass her. Why now? Why should this old song drift through the airport on this of all days? Perhaps I'll tell him about it when I get there, when the plane leaves and he and I are again together.

These people, their feet rubbing away the gloss of the terrazzo floor as they walk swiftly by, believe they have a reason to love. Maybe, but to her they couldn't know how it feels to be needed by one who seems to know her every thought. They wouldn't rush as they do. Individually, they may think they count; individually, they must believe they have good lives—family and friends who love them—but they don't even seem to care about anything. If they had Love, they would surely look it. This is what she sees as her thoughts fade with the music to another time.

He was dashing in his youth, Harold, a lanky young man with jet-black hair. When he smiled, the edge of his left lip would bend down sharply revealing a pleasantly crooked tooth. At least in the beginning, he smiled often, which was comforting to a girl who only a few months earlier turned nineteen. How easy it is to forget such things...the way he turned his head as she walked by, how easy it was to tease him then, and how he used to say, "Lay one on me, baby," when he had enough and wanted a kiss which never

---

1. Orange Colored Sky, written by Milton Delugg and Willie Stein, performed by Nat King Cole and the Stan Kenton Orchestra.

then came soon enough, and usually was followed by many careful caresses. Then his proposal was awkward, in the way Harold rarely was as an older man, a diamond-less ring buried in his left shoe so he wouldn't lose it, which created a circular blister on the ball of his foot as they walked to the restaurant. And her acceptance was immediate, and never regretted.

During the days when the children were young, the trials, the joy—he was always there, a man she could count on. He ensured all Christmases, and birthdays, and any day someone needed attention, got something. And when the day came for him to retire, people came from all around, people he barely remembered, to wish him well. It was a sad day for Harold, and for Olive, to see this man squirm for a purpose again.

"Now boarding flight 79 to Minneapolis, gate number six," comes over the public address system.

Olive looks closely at the ticket that she holds tightly in her hand: "79 to Minneapolis." She realizes her back and legs hurt more than she had ever recalled when she stood and approached the door, and it was farther away than she would have liked. A woman takes part of her ticket and smiles, "Thank You," and points the way to the plane. The jet bridge is chilled, even more than the terminal, and her feet move deliberately, pushing their way toward the plane as if unconnected to the rest of her body.

Inches, inches at a time, her feet slide along the jetbridge carpet. A plane engine screams nearby with breakaway thrust, which momentarily causes her to stop and listen. The handrail is cold and hard and sturdy. The floor is tilted slightly downward and it is difficult to walk on the concentric levels of the telescoping bridge. A man in a hurry passes to her left, following his briefcase. He makes no excuse for his discourteous passing. He smells of sweat through his business suit.

An airport is a loud place. How can a person concentrate on anything? The airplane door is propped open. The paint on the side of the plane is shiny and white yet there are small chips in it, something one doesn't notice unless one looks. There is a smell of cloth and food and perfume, and coffee, and electrical wires and human scent, more so the nearer she approaches the airplane. But it is not offensive; it smells of far away places, of dreams fulfilled. A woman stands, young and beautiful, smiling in her blue uniform, and offers her hand in Olive's direction. At one time she would have refused meekly, but perhaps now…

The world moves in slow motion. She notes her seat and is directed down the aisle. Thoughts move passionately within her head as though she traversed time to another day, a younger day when all life was ahead and there was nothing but the potential for happiness, and love and seeds for memories. Though words are spoken in conversations all around, she understands none; they exist in terms of buzzing only.

Sunshine reflects upon Olive's gray, cloth seat from the adjacent window. Though it is a small space, she is warmed by it when she sits, and her purse finds its way to her side. Then time stands still. She closes her eyes and thinks of Harold.

Only twenty-two feet ahead, the cockpit is in a routine function. The first officer has a foot up on the base of the instrument panel and he has initialized the computer with the flight plan while awaiting the final numbers from the load manifest. He sips a diet soft drink from a plastic cup and thinks about that evening, when his wife is not tired and the kids are asleep, and there is nothing to do but get reacquainted again. It has been four long days since he was home. He takes another slow...deliberate...sip.

A man thrusts a page of numbers at him from just beyond the cockpit door, the load manifest, and he eyes it annoyingly since his daydream had been shattered by such an unexciting task.

"Thanks, buddy," he says.

He runs a pen along columns of numbers verifying the fuel weight, number of passengers, flap setting, weight of the freight in the cargo holds, then stops and takes another sip. All good. He signs it and spins the trim wheel a couple of turns. Task completed, he waves the man away—now to wait for the captain's call for the pushback, time to get back to another connubial daydream.

The heat of the tarmac doesn't bother Harold. There isn't much that bothers him, really. That has always been one of his nicer qualities, his patience, yet the men around him sweat and cuss the heat and are impatient themselves to get back inside the break room to have a soda pop and watch television. They are impatient to push the airplane off the gate and get on with their lives, meaningful lives to them, perhaps, but still not unlike ants.

And Harold waits too. He waits in the darkness where it is one hundred and ten degrees—stifling hot—but he doesn't sweat. And though he is jammed between and underneath 85 suitcases and cardboard boxes, he is not uncomfortable. He doesn't even care that a man, who never excused himself, shoved him in his place, or that two women argued overly loudly next to him, while he rested in a freight cart next to the plane an hour earlier. Harold doesn't care, because he is going home. Nothing else matters—except perhaps, the color of the sky.

Horse Hauler

Come sit right here in our cockpit jumpseat, the little ironing board seat that folds down between circuit breaker panels on the cockpit side of the door. It's been a while, has it? You've never sat in one before? Get comfortable; it can be hard at times. I'll explain: seatbelt straps that go over your shoulders click right into the four point buckle on your belly; the oxygen mask is to your left—don't grab the captain's in case he needs it, he wouldn't like that; the headset is right here; and controls for the audio panel are just above your head on the overhead panel right next to the IRS's. There. Are you comfortable? Good. Going home? It may take a while so you'll have to be patient. Let's just enjoy the show, because this will be interesting.

We push from the gate, ease into the pack, set the brakes, kill our engines and watch.

To the south of us, on the remote corner of the ramp, a horse hauler sits under charcoal skies that fill with electricity. She's an old Boeing 727, a 200 model with a faded paint job that I don't recognize. A girl with a pleasant radio voice is driving it. For the most part, she is quiet there on the cargo section of the airport, not stuck in line as we are. Every flyer's most hated demon, a brewing storm with sinister winds, and lightning, and thunder, slowly inches toward us from the west, shaking the countryside between decreasing pauses. It creeps closer, quietly at first, rumbling softly against our fuselage, making its presence known as sporadic growling in the distant sky.

That dreadful splotch of color smudging our radar analysis map was just to the west of the airport an hour ago, an hour ago when the sun peeked through billowing clouds, when a plane could depart with only minor bending around the fermenting storms, an hour ago when the sky was still amicable.

Another thunderclap—uncomfortably loud.

The control tower, a once friendly bystander, slowly fades away into the mist of the increasing rain. Long ago, a control tower had the luxury of being where it was supposed to be, by the runway, so that the controllers could actually see the airplanes they were supposed to have control over. But in the increasing need to boast that a particular airport has the highest control tower in the neighborhood, the new towers are built far from the action, and so tall that when the weather comes in and the cloud ceiling drops, the tower cab may be the only place on the entire airport where a person can't see a thing. So it becomes a ghostly presence, a phantom in the distance with only a voice that floats within our heads.

Thunder overlaps thunder with almost no peace in between. Blown by the wind, the rain now hisses against us. The sky has progressed to the point of insanity, a normal insanity, and *normal* as in, ordinary, typical, standard, an average happenstance. How often does a storm drift overhead in the summertime? Often. So, we sit under this normal type of insanity, row after row of healthy airliners on the taxiways and ramps, most of us with our engines shut down, filling with a thick, humid air made by the exhalations of hundreds of impatient passengers waiting for the sky to just…relax.

"We'd really like to depart now, we're already thirty minutes behind schedule," says a voice from an opposing airline's plane.

I tilt our radar antenna up and watch as the beam sweeps across the screen revealing a lot of heavy precipitation. The fool. Is he the captain or the first officer of that airplane? Could it be that two competent individuals could come up with the same conclusion, that it is a good idea to go even though the tower closed the airport to departures and is diverting arrivals in this thunderstorm, or has one crewmember made this decision, to go when imprudent? Is one of those pilots mulling over the old adage, "never fly with a person braver than you," and kicking himself for saying nothing, and planning on not flying with the imprudent man in the future? *Just one more leg to go, hurry on through.* How many ended up with that being the last leg ever?

"They say the ride has deteriorated," the phantom tower replies.

"Our radar shows a decent opening if we go right now," says the competitor.

"And he'll be screaming for deviations the second his wheels leave the ground," my own captain says.

"It's better to be on the ground wishing you were in the sky than the other way around," I reply.

A bolt of lightning blasts into the waterlogged earth near the runway and our plane shudders, chatter ceases.

"I wonder if the horses liked that," he says seriously.

I stop counting parked airliners after forty-two, trying to put a price on all of the heavy metal sitting before me. There are two long taxiways parallel to the runways filled with winged jetliners glistening with wetness. The ramps are parking lots. The tower controller says that a tornado was reported not far from us, but it hasn't been confirmed, and I look up to see if I can recognize a telltale vine reaching below the bubbling cloud base. Maybe that one? No, just a random wisp. Over there? No, that too is nothing. I wonder how secure we are out in the open like this. All of these planes could be tossed around like giant toys.

"Not that we could move if we wanted to, but where would you rather be if a tornado struck, here, or in the terminal?" I ask.

He looks around, my captain, whose experience reveals itself through wrinkles, baldness and a sandstone jaw, and scratches his head. "Inside, you would have tons of steel and wood and concrete all around you, but glass everywhere. It's hard to say," he says, tightening his own seatbelt. "We got this metal tube designed for a very rough ride. All of us are strapped in. I'd say we were about as safe as we could be right here."

"True," I reply, and think for a moment how it would feel to be tossed around like little toy Jacks. I guess here is where I'd rather be, strapped in for the ride, and I tighten my seat belt. You should, too.

As the rain pours upon the airport, a seemingly endless supply of water from the sky, it rumbles on our Boeing's fuselage and distorts our view from the cockpit windows. I switch on the wiper momentarily to see this drama, but it disappears once more in a fraction of a second, and we are cocooned, the three of us, in a tiny, cramped cockpit, twisting and rocking while little concentric wavelets rip across the surface in my cup of coffee.

"Okay, now I'm showing a wind direction change," the tower controller says, "that means that I'm going to have to turn this whole airport around." He emphasizes the word *whole*, with his heavy southern drawl as though it was nothing less than the monumental task that it is. And then he begins a succession of thousands of words that take us all from one end of the airport to the other, a long conga line of rocking aluminum. He tells some planes to contact clearance for reroutes around the moving storm cells, others to continue southbound on the taxiway, holding short of intersections, while further telling others to "pass at their own discretion."

The competing airliner complained about the delay again. The horse hauler, whose engines were shut down to conserve fuel, says that she needs to open her enormous cargo door to allow fresh air into the plane, and to give her a *head's up* before she needs to taxi so that she can get buttoned up and restarted.

We start an engine, inch forward a few feet with wipers splashing water to the sides then stop behind another airliner, the one whose tail we have grown intimate with, and then we shut it down again. It'll be awhile before we move. I look over. My partner is speaking into the P.A. microphone, easing thinning nerves with an explanation of our predicament. How long has it been? An hour? Two?

Rain.

Rain is everywhere, charging vertically, horizontally, saturating every leaf of grass, wetting the surface of the earth, floating thousands of fire ants in little pools of mini torrential flood waters, pelting ceaselessly against every stink bug and snake, every robin and sparrow, every inch of muddied earth. Rain. Then lightning appears, strobing, flashing, bolting, ripping razor-like through heaving skies, randomly pricking the earth, blinding and angry. And its brother, thunder, always in disobedience with lightning, is forever brooding, punching, pushing and bullying, a death knell to the ear drum, rattling the viscera and the bones of all living things as they run for cover. Thunder. It shakes and seethes and hates and rumbles, getting wherever it pleases, the far reaches of the most fortified shelter, taunting, taunting, and ever-present in this squall of normal insanity.

Within every statue-like plane, behind two-inch thick glass windshields, behind dozens of complex gauges and dials, behind hundreds of tiny lights that flash when trouble arises, behind an assortment of worn buttons and switches, behind cold metal control wheels, and slouched upon worn sheepskin, rest intrepid men and women of the air—waiting and wondering. Just when is it safe, and who will be the first guinea pig this day? Judging by our position deeply embedded within dozens of airplanes on the taxiway, I sigh profoundly and relax in my seat. Not us. Not us this day.

Lightning flash. Thunder.

"The horses are getting a little antsy," she says.

"I'll bet they aren't as antsy as our lot," another aircraft radios.

"The horses probably smell better though," says another.

"Probably paid more too," says another.

The raindrops sputter, the hissing becomes a mild pitter-pattering on our roof, as the sky calms. It regains its composure in between giant squall lines, but I am not fooled. Even though the rain recedes, menacing clouds lurk off in the distance. I know it isn't finished with us yet.

"Okay, now they tell me that there wasn't actually a tornado earlier," says the tower.

"Then can we go?" says the foolish competitor, slicing the end off the controller's words. There is no response.

We are all in line facing the new runway, a linear audience watching a production enacted upon the real world. We see through the wide expanse of the windshield, hear through the countless microprocessors within our radios, note the wind and rain, and watch, patiently, patiently as the very real and usual drama of airline flying unfolds before us. I only wish that our payload can hear all that we do, and see, and feel, for if they could, not a fingernail would go unbit at the first site of the tiny lights that fade into view beyond the runway threshold. Just one set of lights pushing through the rain, floating high then low, a wing dips and then straightens. To us it floats casually, a wagging wing here, a yawing nose there, but to those who are in the plane, wagging and yawing feels just like a ride on the big, black Spider in an amusement park, except only the pilot's perspiring hands are all that hold everything together against the cantankerous wind.

The tower clears him to land.

The new guinea pig manages a "Roger."

He comes in sporadically at first, a big jet airliner probably shy on fuel and, but for this one chance, moments away from a divert. He nestles snuggly within the navigational confines of his electronic glideslope, but that doesn't last for long as a gust of wind blows him high and then the wind changes and he maneuvers abruptly to regain his decent. Then he's low, too low. A tail gust? More power! More power! I mouth. Is he going to make it?

He flies higher, then too high. It looks like he's going around! But no, he regains equanimity moments before touch down. He floats, floats, floats farther than I am sure he wanted to, then...chops the power and slams hard. Buckets open wide; engines suck in funnels of standing water from the runway.

"We had plus or minus twenty," says the harried voice of the guinea pig. "A rough ride all the way down."

"Sorry about that," the tower phantom says, as though he was responsible for the misbehaving sky, then gives a thousand more words of instructions to the rest of us.

"Tower, we had a few windshear alerts holding short of the runway."

"Who said that?"

"We did," another airliner interjects, "we had two windshear alerts squawking at us as that other plane was landing."

Nothing was said for an uncomfortable amount of time as dozens of pilots fidget in anticipation while they wait for a response.

"Interesting...I had none," says the phantom tower. "I'm closing off all arrivals then."

Lightning, thunder.

"Holy smokes, it's moving in again," captain says.

The thunder returns more abruptly than the first time, beating into us. The ragged base of the storm twists in the sky above us. Little tendrils of slate colored wisps twirling in the wind breeze by; mockingly brushing the treetops, relieving them of a few weakened leaves. Gradually the sound of rain increases from a mild pitter-patter, to a maddening hiss, then to the roar of pea sized hail. And lightning flashes in random strobes from every direction. We are in it again, and again I wonder if it is selfish for pilots to enjoy this natural production safely on the ground as our passengers sit patiently losing any resemblance of a traveling plan. This is what we do, what we longed for in our quest for a seat in the front of a big airliner: to be a part of the majesty of aviation, on the ground as well as in the air; to see and understand the world of the aviator, the airliner, the wind, and rain.

"We have a little dilemma," says a plane somewhere in the middle of the pack. "If we don't get airborne soon, we are going to have to return to the gate to get some air to a dog in the baggage pit."

"Yeah, we have a dog too," says another. "You might as well put us in for a gate return too."

I figure at least ten percent of the airplanes sitting in this storm must have at least one pet in their cargo holds. To shuffle us around so that they can be pulled out of the lineup and allow the critters a little fresh air at the gate will create a great confusion, but then that's what ground controllers are for, untying an ever-tightening knot.

"Alrighty," says the phantom, unfazed, welcoming the challenge as though he meant to say, "Bring it on. Is that the best you got?" We become old couples in checkered shirts doe-si-doeing in a square dance. Somehow in all the perceived confusion of the many moving planes, as we turn away from each other and go down parallel taxiways, wait some more, change directions as others split from the group and ease back in, the impatient competitor ends up somewhere far into the back of the pack, so far back that I can't even tell what type of plane he is. As we change positions, being readjusted in a way that only a masochistic air traffic controller can keep track of, the downpour gradually ceases, and only distant echoes of thunder remain. For the first time this day, I put on my sunglasses as a little beam that winks through a cloudy crack above seems blinding compared to the crushing dreariness of the importunate cloud cover. Oh so delightful it is! This little beam of release from the torment, let us bask in your splendor; go forth and multiply my friend, fill the sky with your brethren. Tell them all that they are welcome. I see! Here they come!

Things move in a good way for a change. I see life renewed toward the front of the line as airliners slowly start up again with little puffs of gray smoke from their engines. They burn again with eager thrust, each engine twisting reality, bending light behind it with their ejected heat. Bending reality to the flighted aviator's world now, not the grounded one, as the horse hauler makes her wide turn onto the runway. Her large cargo door is now securely buttoned up and she aims toward a more relaxed sky. Smoke belches from her three spooled engines, her brakes release; she gains speed toward us as we sit and admire the grace of a patient jet plane crew rotating abeam us, skyward into the vast beyond.

A Good Pilot

Buffalo can be an unforgiving place. It sits in a damp, peculiar valley abutting Lake Erie, the roaring Niagara lying just to the north. It is one of the relatively few places on earth susceptible to a phenomenon called *Lake Effect*, wherein temperamental stratus hovers persistently by the whims of an unrelenting wind off the lake—like *Peanuts* character Charlie Brown's ubiquitous cloud of depression. The air is frequently clammy, rain or shine. Even the birds huddle closely together under brown winter leaves trying to escape the incessant cold, just like factory workers in the local bar.

The city is filled with those who never left for better skies. Its inhabitants are rough and tumble, used to the weather and all its tribulations, and callous to the constant supply of bad news that accompanies such a place. Which is why, not long ago, hardly a soul noticed a small pile of twisted aluminum found a few yards away from a busy highway one very gray, Sunday morning.

The wreckage was scattered in a clump of mangled shards of aluminum and torn seat cushions, barely recognizable as the kind of plane that dots many a local airfield, eliciting happier thoughts of flight. Most don't know the pilot of this plane, or what events led up to its final connection with the earth this moldering day. But what is known, is that the man whose body lies in an equally indiscriminate clump nearby *was* a pilot, a man who believed he was doing a prudent thing until something happened in which he was ultimately unprepared.

A number of things could have happened along the way. A plane such as this has no de-icing capability. Perhaps being caught above the cloud deck, and with little fuel left to circumnavigate it, he was forced through it, accumulating more ice than the little airplane could handle. It was a risk he had to take once he found himself engulfed in the Lake Effect. Perhaps his fate was determined the minute his sole engine sputtered and quit and he found himself drifting through the fog only to meet the ground just a second after recognizing it. Perhaps his instrument flying skills were not up to par, an affliction many instrument rated pilots have who rarely use them, or that he may have had an undeserved confidence in his ability to maintain spatial orientation, something pilots get when all they see is blue sky and meandering prominences on a clear, summer day. Regardless of what occurred on this fateful day, the risks he took put him in a condition beyond his control, a manner in which no pilot could ever survive.

The notion of a *good pilot* is often mistaken. Some say that the one who can handle intensely stressful conditions, while barely batting an eyelash, is a good pilot. Some say that he who can predictably *kiss the earth* as though landing on a carpet of silk every time is a good pilot. And even some believe, strangely, that the one who aims to clip the red in a thunderstorm and survive, is a good pilot. These people are more correctly labeled as *lucky*.

Across the Cayuga river valley, at the airport, fire trucks position themselves facing each other abeam the entrance to the ramp, and turn on their hoses forming a grand arc ahead of an oncoming plane. They are not saluting a retiring *lucky* pilot, they are saluting a *good* one, because no one lasts for thirty years of flying airplanes by relying solely on luck. It isn't about smooth hands and greasy landings, or being personable or demanding. It is about risk and how they manage it, and there are many risks in aviation still, though those who are ignorant may disagree. All of the automation found on flight decks, the autopilots, the precise navigation systems, auto throttles and auto brakes serve the purpose of making life, and skills, dull. As we deal with the treacheries of Mother Nature, all of this automation can't keep up in intense turbulence. The risk still and forever will be the pilot-in-command's. He is the one who is responsible for the hundreds of lives resting on his fingertips as everything else decides to quit.

Lou sits in the left seat, an older man with a pallid shimmer in his hair, the four gold stripes on his shoulders are faded with time to a more brownish color. On any other day he shows little emotion, but today, this day of retirement, his eyes appear to float in little pools of water on either side of his nose. He stares straight ahead at the arc formed between the two big trucks, and cannot speak, yet thinks back to the choices he made with his life. Each day he made many. He thinks of the thousands of people he took to the airways, loved ones to someone mostly, and how he settled them back to the ground to continue on with their lives. They trusted him implicitly, not knowing that he had devoted his life to keeping them safe from the dangers that they will never know or understand.

Lou, the *captain* as he had been labeled, could easily have courted risk along the way, as some pilots occasionally do. At one point in his earlier years, he could have flown single engine airplanes in all types of conditions, not unlike the *unlucky pilot* by the highway. And there is nothing illegal about it. He could have flown over the mountains of Colorado at night, or over low Lake Effect clouds hiding rime ice in a single engine airplane. The inherent chance of catastrophe should that one engine give up is far greater, the risk—far greater, than the route *he* chose to go with his life. The same goes for the many times he added that little extra amount of fuel when his gut told him to expect more than the average amount of delays along the east coast.

He always took the conservative path when the time came to head for the bad weather, to judge the reliability of the plane he flew, and even which company he chose to work for. These decisions he knew, ultimately afforded him the chance to slowly taxi his big jet plane toward the arcing beams of water, and not end up by the highway.

The clouds at first parted like cracks in glass, then slowly give way to a sun-soaked blue. Distant maple branches teeter back and forth by the urging of the wind. To the northeast, beyond the flight line, amongst the fresh, white, melting snow, a farm nestles in the lap of the hills of the Tonawanda. The arc of water stands as a monument on the ramp, a gateway to a new life. The jet plane rolls slowly toward it. Water discharges upward from the fire truck nozzles, a reflection to the downward charge of the nearby Niagara. It is an extraordinary arc of water, an extraordinary honor for this man to be the recipient of such a tribute as the spray tinkles upon the windshield, then tinkles on the cabin, and then, as the wings cross the arc they are wetted too.

Lou wants to set the brakes before crossing entirely through, and he slows the plane down noticeably while he thinks about it. To cross the threshold is not the end, but the beginning of a life void of the necessity of striving to minimize risk in every moment. How does one live like that? He thinks. It's like a man spending a lifetime hoarding money for retirement, then having to spend it to live—it is a very difficult thing to do.

The plane eases through, and Lou hears faint applause from beyond the cockpit door.

Sage Advice from 35,000 Feet

"If there's anything you need to remember, it's never to wear your watch when you go out walking on an overnight."

I always wear my watch. If I leave it in my room, there is that possibility I may forget it there just as I have a hundred pairs of sunglasses.

"Why?"

"Let me tell you about a time I went out for my usual walk about town. I don't remember the city, it could have been any one of them, they are all the same after a while, you know..."

"Yes."

"Well, anyway, it's like this," he said, taking his attention away from the instruments long enough to corner me with his eyes. "You know I tend to walk wherever I go. I can't stand taking a taxi. I like to go whenever I please, stop along the way and check places out. But it sometimes gets me into trouble. One minute I'm walking in a perfectly good neighborhood, then—and it isn't like this in the country or suburbs—the next minute I'm smack dab in the middle of a perfectly lousy neighborhood."

"I hate that."

"Damn straight. Sometimes I get so caught up in my own thoughts that when I really take a moment to look around I find that I am deep into this ghetto with winos coming up to me asking for change, and, strange as it sounds, asking for the time. Of course, I figure they want the watch at that point, but they just ask the time and go their own way." He lifts his wrist and shakes the face of his cheap watch toward me. "I'm not one to wear one of those fancy Rolex's like some guys do; you've got to give me credit for that."

"No fancy watches."

"More than that. So there I was again, picking up my pace through this run down area when sure enough, a guy lying against a trash can yells, 'Hey Mister, do you know what time it is?' You got to know that this was about the tenth time a wino had asked me the time that day, and I was getting fed up with it pretty quick. I just wanted to get out of there, find a place to send an email and grab a little steak."

"So what'd you do?"

"I went up to the guy, lying there in a torn, greasy, avocado colored leisure suit coat, wearing pants that smelled like they hadn't been changed since 1979, and I said clearly and succinctly, 'What the hell do *you* need to know the time for? It's not like you have any place to go.' I mean, I was genuinely interested in knowing why these people kept asking me the time. Was I missing out on something? Maybe the city passed out free vodka at some precise time, but I doubted it."

"Do you think that that guy just wanted your watch?"

"Hold on there, I'm getting to it. So he stands up immediately and points his snot-stained finger in my face and goes off on me. He says: 'That's just what I expected out of the likes of you! You come here into my neighborhood with your fancy combed hair and shoes and shirt and all, and expect us to not have lives too. Well, I'll tell you, mister moneybags, I got things to do! I got places to be, I got people to meet, why, I probably got more things to do than you there, chump. Just because I choose not to wear one of them there fancy watch things don't mean that I don't need to know the time. Hell, why don't you just get out of here. I'll find the time from somebody else, someone who doesn't look down his nose at us, someone who cares about people, someone I can call brother.'"

"I was taken aback for sure. He had a point. Who was I to expect that just because someone appeared down and out that they really didn't have places to be? I suppose he *could* have been a fairly upstanding individual on a peculiar dinner break, one who never changed his pants."

"What happened, what happened?"

"So feeling bad, I told him it was seven o'clock. And he says: 'Fine...fine. Thank you. Now was that so hard?' 'No,' I said, and I apologized for prejudging him. And then do you know what he said?"

"I can't imagine."

"He said, 'Is that AM or PM?'"

It Only Happens Once Each Year

The Boeing levels off somewhere high in a powder blue sky over Indiana. It is headed south, full of passengers who sit quietly, read and sleep. The sound of wind against the fuselage becomes lesser up at the flight levels where, though the mach speed increases, the airspeed decreases. So it is quiet, except for the mumbling of one exasperated man in a white shirt with his head tilted back and eyes darting under closed lids. A woman in a green cashmere sweater, sitting across the aisle from him, places her book in her lap for a moment and listens to faint words from his lips. She hears: "max throttle, positive rate, and gear up." She is curious, so she listens and watches intently, but tries not to stare.

His left hand moves forward then back again as his fingers pinch invisible levers, then places them carefully into an invisible notch. His right hand makes a fist around an invisible control wheel and is pulled toward his chest. A bell is chiming somewhere in the cabin and the aroma of peanut breath from a hundred chewing mouths fills the air.

"Oxygen masks and regulators on, one hundred percent," he mumbles, "crew communications establish!" He reaches up and flips invisible switches. "No smoke and seatbelt signs on."

She wonders what he is doing. Is he hallucinating? Why is this man talking to himself? She assumes that he is just another traveling lunatic and focuses her attention onto the video screen that just opened in front of her.

In the man's mind—

The fire bell screams and the left engine gauges die. "Engine fire!"

"You have the airplane."

"Okay, I got it. Engine fire checklist."

"Center, we're declaring an emergency," he radios, "and will need to drift down to a lower altitude." The autopilot clicks off and the alarm goes: "baap, baap, baap!"

"Fire handle number one verify."

"Verify."

"Pulling number one engine fire handle. Extinguisher engage."

"Engage."

"Apu start and on bus…"

"The fire's not out!"

She is a little bit annoyed, sitting there across from him as she chews on her own peanuts, though she tries to look away, though his behavior just doesn't make sense. He seems normal, groomed appropriately, not like a typical destitute mumbler like the kind that the lower airfares seem to attract. A flight attendant walks down the aisle asking for trash and thanks people for it.

"Excuse me?" the woman asks, and points to the man in the trance, "can you explain?"

The flight attendant looks for a moment at the man with the darting hands and rolls her eyes. She looks at his clothes, his shiny, black shoes, his haircut. "Yes," she says, as though she has seen men like him a hundred times before, "He's one of ours."

"One of yours?"

"Well, yes, you see that book on the seat next to him is a flight manual, and those are index cards in his right hand, most likely filled with numbers he's supposed to know all the time, and his clothes look new off the rack. Those are sure signs that he's on his way to a pilot proficiency check. They have those once a year, you know."

"A pilot?"

"I'm afraid so. They get that way sometimes."

"Hmm."

"Trash?"

"Yes," she says tossing the last nut in her mouth, "just a peanut bag."

"Thank you."

She watches him for a moment, and listens, the woman in the seat. It is more pleasing to hear, not so peculiar, now. She listens to him repeat airplane words, emergency words, calmly pushing imaginary things in front of him. It makes sense that one should have to study continuously to fly a plane. How could one just learn everything there is to know once without forgetting? Yes, one who studies is one who is prepared. Pilots must pretend and relearn constantly, whatever that may be, to "*dry fly*" the maneuver so that it will come as a second nature for him in an actual emergency. She wonders why this never occurred to her before, that once a thing is learned it is never practiced, never forgotten.

Let him do more, let him make all the noises and movements he wants to, she thinks, I want to see that he knows, let him fret over there in the seat as he mumbles "generator failure," and "rapid decompression," so that I don't have to. Let him move his hands confidently about the row of seats, dousing flames and landing without flaps, and navigating without electricity.

Let him.

She kicks off her shoes and feels the cool carpet under her feet.

And first officer Simon opens his eyes.

Done. That's it—I am done studying, he thinks. He looks over at the lady in the green sweater as she sleeps in the next row.

There was a time whenever he approached his once a year annual simulator proficiency check, that he began to acquire unexplained symptoms of illness such as a psychosomatic backache or heartburn that wouldn't go away. There was a time not so long ago. And no matter how well they disguise the current annual testing and oral reviews into touchy-feely *get togethers*, he still agonizes over appearing the fool, especially during the last few days prior to the event. So he studies a little too much maybe and frets a little too much until the assessment is over, because it is his only chance each year to prove to his employer that he knows his stuff and is worth his pay, aside from surviving a real crisis. So, like so many pilots, he even studies during his flight to the city where the simulator lurks.

He hopes that no one notices.

Zen and the Dash 8

We stand here by the counter while the last of the passengers trickle through the door, my twelve-year-old son, Danny, and I. A lady holding a cherub-esque pink baby is one of the last to board before they clear us on too.

"We'll be sitting next to that little bugger you can be sure," I say. And though the infant is cute and bright-eyed, with its little head bobbing with every movement of his mother's pheasant-like breasts, I know that the moment they close the cabin door of the Dash-8 he will decide that he doesn't want to travel anymore. Like a magnet, those types of carry-ons always seem to find me no matter which seat I get.

From my window, I see that LaGuardia is bustling as usual. Its ramps and taxiways are filled like a slow moving traffic jam with airliners of varying colors during this late afternoon bank. Our plane is mostly full with an extraordinarily high number of backpack toters, but a few are also business people itching to get home to their New England town. As we inch toward the runway end, as suspected, the mother and infant are sitting the next row over, and I sense with his first peep, and then the next, and next in closer succession, that he is winding up for a grand crying fest.

"Dad, can I have my comic book?" Danny asks.

"Sure," I say, and then lean forward, dig into my carry-on suitcase and take out his little magazine. I hand it to him.

"Thanks," he says, opens it, and begins savoring the pictures.

I read my own book, too, in an effort to divert my attention from the baby noises close by. The baby's mother "coos" frustratingly, sounding as though she wishes that she could comfort him, and the rest of us, better. She is probably thinking that the rest of us are preparing ourselves for another one of those "flights from hell" with a screaming child dominating the cabin for the entire flight. She's right of course, I hate to think. Sitting here, I am thankful that Danny is beyond that. But I remember those times when he was younger and we went on some unavoidable flights and I couldn't control his natural baby tendency to cry when he had had enough. I remember feeling bad for all the others on board, because I knew how they felt, and there was nothing I could do about it no matter how hard I tried. I look over at Danny sitting there now, and realize how lucky I am that he doesn't do that anymore.

We acquire the runway sooner than I expected. Three chimes sound as the little Dash 8 lines up to the west. As the pilot applies take-off power, I realize that I had forgotten how loud Dash 8's are, drowning out almost all but the crying baby sounds. It is a powerful groan, an all encompassing roar of low pitched propeller power, a jaw quivering warble of unsyced propellers, as he lets go of the brakes and we hurry down the runway. We accelerate quickly, the lightness of the little airplane allowing it to gain speed fast and my back fills my seat. Sparkles from Bowery Bay glisten just beyond our windows. Danny turns a page of his comic book.

To those who fly jets, it seems as though we are too slow to become airborne, but we are...rotating slowly into the air, the wheels folding forward into their nests beneath the engine nacelles. Slowly, slowly we float over the East River, the tall buildings of Manhattan becoming clearer as we bank to the right, the Chrysler building, the Empire State, and I look down on the long, long green meadows of Central Park with little dots of people below. I know the routine up in the cockpit. Air traffic control is handing us off like a baton in a relay race, turning us to avoid other airplanes from other airports, keeping us slow and low at times, then urging us to climb as fast as we can to get out of their airspace. Bank a little to the right, bank a little to the left, lower nose, raise nose, propeller noise becoming more baritone with the reduction to climb power.

There is highway traffic below, long lines of vehicles exiting the city packing the George Washington Bridge with trucks, mostly. The little pink baby is entering the realm of total discomfort and he is letting everyone else know, all of us with our noses buried in books regardless of how impossible it is for us to concentrate on what we are reading. We read without comprehending, appearing as though we don't care, as though we are unaffected by the sounds of the little bugger, and can control our every thought and action regardless of what goes on around us. But who are we fooling? I lose track of the story as each cry mingles with the written word. I close my book and look out the window, across from Danny, trying to think of anything but the bawling little infant, concentrating hard on anything but his relentless crying.

We are in a Dash 8, a well-built airplane of distinguished style. She's short on the inside but rugged on the outside—as any would expect a Canadian-built airplane to be—a living thing, really, with a unique personality even prior to the addition of the pilots and passengers. And like all living things, she has two distinct sides that make up her *essence*, or that which we refer to as *this particular airplane*. She's made up of two parts: first, the practical, technical, *left brained* components, consisting of electrical systems, hydraulic systems and fuel systems, further broken down to propeller gear box drive mechanisms connecting through a spline to generators, then generator control units, voltage regulators, wiring, separate buses and then to individual components through circuit breakers. The fuel system is broken down to tanks, electric and engine driven pumps (connected through another spline), check valves, crossfeed valves, filters and heat exchangers into a hydro-mechanical unit that regulates fuel flow into the burner cans and igniters. The hydraulic system is broken down into separate components made up of engine driven, and/or electrically driven pumps that supply 3000 psi pressurized purple Skydrol by way of reservoirs through piping to actuators that operate spoilers, flaps, and rudder flight controls, being manipulated by either the captain's side control wheel or the first officer's, through a connecting shaft with a disconnect clutch. And there are quite a few other systems making up the practical, technical aspects of that which we call this *airplane*.

There are many Dash 8's, all built to these same specifications, with the same components, yet they all still have their own unique personalities through distinct experiences of hard landings, worn bell cranks and leaky actuators from years of use. They have developed their own unique flying feel or personality…sometimes docile and forgiving, or cranky and abrasive. And there is a love that we develop for a particular machine, due in part to the experiences we shared within it. This is true for all machines, and living things, which brings up the other aspect: the second, the visceral, spiritual or *right brained* part of the machine that completes the whole unit. Without these two sides, the object is merely an object and not the object of our desire. It wouldn't be something that sparks us with a feeling of joy when we see it, when we use it, when we experience life through it.

We humans, not unlike this airplane, are made up of dozens of systems that make up the whole. Without the synchronous operation of our systems, we cease to operate, or to function as an entity. Without the spiritual, right-brained, or second half of this equation, like the airplane, we would be just a container for various useless inoperative accoutrements. We have components that must work in unison not unlike this Dash 8. For instance, our digestive system, like the fuel system of the airplane, takes food/fuel through mastication in the mouth, then down the esophagus, then stomach, where it is mixed with gastric juices and through peristalsis forced into the duodenum, then into the small intestine where the food/fuel is absorbed into the blood and lymph system. The blood delivers this fuel/energy to our muscles or the airplane equivalent of engines and hydraulic systems, to our nervous system, our lungs or the equivalent electrical system and pneumatic system. That is the practical, technical, operational side of our animal bodies, something we share with machines, but to be human we must also take into account that which has no physical substance but what makes up the non-ethereal essence of *us*. It is the second half, the half that only works when the practical stuff operates normally, it is what happens when our master switch is switched on and we are powered up.

We share a spirit that is the product of the many elements within our body working in harmony together. The spirit of "us" comes alive when our theoretical propellers begin to turn, when our gyros spin and align, when our radios squawk and our actuators pump flight controls up and down. And when we take to the air—that's when we are alive. That's what I see sitting here in this machine as we hum at what I imagine is somewhere near eighteen thousand feet over the tree-lined farms of Connecticut.

And what about us, here, now, we passengers? I look around, nearly every seat is full. No one talks, no one communicates, except for the baby. We all just have our heads facing forward in some fashion feigning reading, feigning life, merely machines operating on autopilot with our lives on hold until we are beyond this place with the miserable, relentless crying. We are right now merely containers for our systems, dull-eyed zombies lacking spirit. We sit next to, but do not regard, the persons next to us, enduring life for as long as necessary until we regain control again, surrounded by our own peace and able to continue as whole persons.

Danny is engrossed in his comic book. Without taking his eyes from the pages, he reaches down on the floor by his left foot and brings up a pacifier that must have fallen, and hands it to the baby's mother.

She thanks him, cleans the end off with her blouse, and feeds it to her baby.

And he stops crying.

When Snow Flies in San Diego

It is definitely there, the odor of campfire smoke, of charred oak or maple or mesquite, all at once in a wash of mixed memories, of happy times of camping in Vermont along the shores of Lake Champlain on a misty Autumn morning, or alluding to the weeks that Yellowstone burned, setting the western sky ablaze over a decade ago. But the wheel well? Why do I inhale this odor in the wheel well of our 737 a thousand miles from any major fire? I can understand burned rubber, or plastic, the splattered tar from a hot runway, or of hot glycol, but campfire smoke?

I report my findings to the captain.

"Are you sure that it isn't because we are headed toward San Diego and you have wild fires on the brain?" he says. "This plane just landed a few minutes ago, flew with three hundred mile per hour wind against it for hours, sucking away at anything down there, blowing...cleansing it of any contaminated odors. Are you sure?"

"Yes."

I pull out the logbook. "Look."

He stares at it for a while with a demanding look. "I'll be damned; it just *came* from San Diego. That means that odor stayed with the plane the whole way."

"Just exactly how bad is this fire over there?" I say, "I mean, these planes fly in all kinds of smog, and moldy climates, and we haul all kinds of pungent cargo—an occasional box of tuna that gets a little ripe and lingers for a little while—but to stick to the *outside* of the plane for so many miles, just how bad is it over there?"

He snaps the metal covered book shut. "Bad."

As I walk through the terminal, I catch glimpses of the news streaming from the big television monitors hanging from the ceiling. Small crowds of passengers gather around them to see footage of the inferno inching its way toward neighborhoods that may be their own. They look at their watches more nervously than usual, hoping beyond hope that their flight doesn't cancel as literally hundreds already have from other airlines with large bases in California. I can tell by the universal look of concern on their faces that they are desperate to tend to their own emergencies. A groan erupts from the group surrounding the television; a man comes up to me while the others look on.

"They just reported that all flights going into San Diego have been cancelled," he says.

All of a sudden I feel perplexed. I hate that. We just talked to a dispatcher who said we were still going. Now I have to determine who has their finger on the pulse of the situation more accurately—our dispatcher, or a national news organization. I hate to appear unknowing in front of the passengers, especially since we were about to fly them, by all accounts, into the vicinity of hell's inferno. I decide to go with my gut, to trust the folks who so many times steered me right.

"Don't believe everything you see on T.V.," I say. "We'll get you there." I board my plane.

Concern is ever-present. Not only are the passengers concerned, but the mothers and fathers of our flight attendants as well. They called throughout the four-day trip asking their daughters if their flights to southern California had been cancelled. They heard the news of firestorms raging throughout California and their imaginations went wild with thoughts of their little darlings running for their lives the moment our airplane's wheels touched the California pavement. We are going, of course. It isn't the *cancel at the drop of a hat* 1980's, after all. As their pilot, I think about conveying calm with every word I speak, assuring them and our passengers that the fires are many miles from downtown and the airport, and we will never put them in a position that isn't safe; it may be uncomfortable, but not unsafe.

Ironically, parents of pilots generally don't call. If the folks are still alive, they have grown callous to the concerns of their sons and daughters safety after years of thunderstorms and hurricanes and windy mountains, and madmen with box cutters. Pilot's parents don't call to enquire if flights are cancelled anymore for sanity's sake. Our job, we all know, is to find a way. That's really why we get paid, especially in these lean times, not to play with a fifty million dollar piece of equipment on a magnificent summer afternoon with air so smooth that any monkey can fly it. We get paid to find a way to our destination.

We board and take to the skies, now, amidst a solemn mood. It isn't like any normal flight. There is a couple on board who lost their house while they were on vacation, some cruise. The babysitter luckily took their children out of the house before it was engulfed in flames and burned into a pile of cinders. That's what they tell me as we point this plane toward the smoke that is gathering high over eastern places like Phoenix.

We see things on television, things happening in the world. We see these things while we sit on our couch in a comfortable robe while sipping hot tea. We have solid walls around us, soft carpet at our feet, maybe a dog's head resting on our thigh as we sip and watch the world go by. But pilots of the line see things differently; maybe it's why we do the job. One day we are on that couch just like everybody else; the next, duty calls us to be there, where the action is, to evacuate refugees from Bosnia; to bring help to a flood ravaged Mexico; September 11th firefighters to Ground Zero; soldiers to the Middle East. And one-time homeowners to fire scorched California while the fires still blaze, so that they can claim their rubble. We see it. We are part of this world, not just observers sometimes.

As we begin our descent out over the Salton Sea, we face a wall of sooty air hovering over the fire-speckled ridges. I have never witnessed the effects of napalm after it had been dropped in a war, but my eyes tell me that this is what it's like. It could be any war, but mostly it could be just another view of Iraq, as we near from the desert side of the mountains, treeless for the most part until a few miles farther west, then thick woods tolerate fires so large that I can clearly see them from many miles away, filling the air with plumes of smoke. And from so far away, smoke is all that I can see from horizon to horizon, all the way down, deep into Mexico. We are both awestruck, the captain and I. We make comments of war and the kinds of battles that are won and lost down there among the firefighters and tanker pilots.

Tragedy doesn't elicit thoughts of sorrow from a television set. But once we see and experience the loss of real people, who happened to be sitting a few feet behind us on this airplane, one can't help but become introspective. Are we doing enough?

Brown smoke licks the belly of our 737 the way a rapist licks. Knowing its destruction of what lay below causes me to shudder. Immediately this butterfly in which we are flying is cocooned in a blanket so thick that the sun is immediately lost. My eyes begin to water while an occasional cough erupts from otherwise silent passengers behind our door, people who would have never expected to know what it felt like to float through such sooty air only a week ago. We are handed off between SOCAL controllers who are working with backup systems, because the fires threatened their domain. And, true to their professionalism, give us a perfect heading that allows us to intercept the localizer to runway two-seven, taking us just over that bothersome parking garage just off the approach end of it. We continue down. Down through the choking smoke, in eerily calm air. The wings barely jostle. There, I see, through the lightening haze, the symmetric structures of the city, the freeway, the parking garage. One mile out and little white approach lights appear to guide our way toward the ghost of two-seven. And I see, as we near, something I have never seen before in southern California. It wasn't unusual to see snow in northern climes, but there? Has hell frozen over?

"Three hundred feet."

I wonder if this is damaging to the plane.

"Two hundred feet."

But it was beautiful, in a way.

"One hundred feet."

Ash, floating all around.

"Decelerating through 80 knots."

Look at them. They are all wearing masks.

Prima Donnas

Whether or not a pilot belongs to a union, there seems to always be discord between management and pilots, an *us verses them* mentality. The cause is undoubtedly due to a lack of communication, one group believing the other has an undeserved advantage.

I do not *dislike* airline management. I can't, because an airline manager put food on my table and a roof over my head. An airline manager changed my diaper, taught me how to play *pick-up-sticks* and how to win at chess. An airline manager bought me my first bike. He left the house five days a week at 7:00 o'clock in the morning and came home twelve hours later (sometimes on weekends) to secure his precarious job. And, contrary to what many pilot's think, airline managers do not make the kind of money that pilots do. An airline manager told me that anyway, as he gulped down a cup of tepid, black coffee and hurried out the door...

Some nights he'd come home discouraged, because something didn't work right at work. A deal he'd been negotiating fell through or someone played dirty politics that day, as they tend to do in an office environment. And he would sit in his chair and pour himself a drink to forget about it.

"Those pilots," he'd say, "got it good. Those prima donnas sit back and let the automation take them to their destination in those sweet machines, get their coffee served hot by little princesses all day long. Got those fat contracts. Don't do what I do, kid," he would say. "Be a pilot. Life is easy when you are a pilot."

That's what I remember anyhow as we drift down just under the ragged base of these damn serious clouds. Our engines accelerate and decelerate by the command of my throttles as they are punched and pulled, eased up, and then eased back, thwarting gusts. Rain hisses against us through black-ened drapes of water under the cumulous as we go in and out of them. At once, there is only gray beyond our windows…then I see the little black runway…and then it disappears in the grayness. Then, fuzzy flashing ODALS (Omni Directional Approach Lighting System), draw us in like a lighthouse does a ship on a stormy sea. We are heaving in this wind as the heat from below pushes up the air and rain—and us—through this south Florida wetness that has dominated the sky most of the past summer. And I am exhausted though I don't know it yet, because I am running on adrenaline.

One's mind thinks about many things when they fly around Florida thunderstorms—our motivations, for instance. Why play with these storms, in this place, the seeming source for all of the world's bad weather? Training tells us never to go near one, but we cannot ground these airplanes for months at a time just because Florida is having an unusually stormy summer. They were pepper dots on long-range radar that grew in size the nearer we came, as if growing to meet us in a fistfight, then into waves of fury racing us to the airport. So we become a gazelle, chased by tigers, as a means for our own survival.

So here I am, thinking about what my airline manager said while I am now on the run.

Our wings tilt down to the left around another cell, then to the right, on an intercept course back toward the runway. We descend clumsily down the glideslope, this metal Boeing tube filled with mommas, and babies, and working folk—managers too—our approach speed wavering, wavering in the wind, wavering in the sky above the swamps and highways. Throttles jostle to keep up as we jolt by an irritated Mother Nature, her blackness and flashings are everywhere, from the south toward Miami, and toward the north, not far from Orlando. It is the same: big, fat, cumulonimbus, repeating, line after line, pushing across the state—as usual. And, as we encountered them, even though we flew fifty miles out over the gulf, far away from our intended route, we still were negligibly beaten.

The ground becomes more clearly visible as we descend and our dwindling fuel quantity is a consideration. I see the faint smoke trail of an MD-80 in the sky below, a speck seemingly hovering between us and the runway on a ham-fisted approach. We are to follow him. He has not touched down…Yet.

"Reduce to your final approach speed now," the tower controller stabs the radio waves, sounding as though he is trying to keep his Tourette's syndrome in check. "I've got another plane to depart between you and the pre-ceding aircraft."

Another plane between us?

"You know how I feel about that, don't you?"

I look perplexedly toward my captain. "That it's going to be too tight!"

"Like that BB king song: Nobody loves me but my momma, and she might be jivin' too."

"Gawd. I'm making an S turn to the left."

"Touch down already...Slowpoke!"

Make your turn-off, make it quick, or it's back up into those damn seri-ous clouds...And we are already going as slow as we can go.

Nine hundred feet.

The MD-80's wheels make little white puffs of smoke as it touches down. *Good. Make the turn off. Make it. Was that lightning over there? He missed the turn off.*

Dammit.

"If we miss the approach, the chart says to maintain runway heading. That will take us straight into that cell directly ahead."

"Then we go left around it," the captain says.

"There, he's making the turn off."

Seven hundred feet.

I'm ready on the TOGA (Take Off Go Around) switches. Ready on the go-around, but I'm more ready to get the hell down. Storms not far, just to the southwest moving northeast...toward the field, another straight ahead. *How do those calls go again? Press TOGA switches, flaps fifteen, check power, positive rate...gear up, set missed approach altitude. Okay, there, got that square in my mind...best not forget though; it'd be assholes and elbows for sure—if—it comes to a go-around, to go back up in that...smoldering sky.* Another airplane rolls into position on the runway and the tower clears him for an immediate take off. I hear thunder over the standard airplane noises.

"So, if that guy's cleared for immediate take off, why is he moving so slow?"

Five hundred feet.

"C'mon, rotate, you."

Quickly now!

Two hundred feet.

They cleared him for an immediate left turn around the storm cell after take off. If we have to go around that would put him directly below us. Our choice is either to go directly into that huge cell as per the chart instructions, or directly over him as he climbs to the left on take off. *Jesus, things can go to hell in a hand basket quickly up here.*

"Get ready to go around."

My fingers delicately fondle the switches that will point us back up into the sky and give us a go-around power setting. My left hand is ready to shove throttles, my right ready to pull the control wheel. The captain's fingers are ready on the flap handle, but we both dread it. If...he doesn't get off the ground in a hurry.

Fifty feet...

Rotate, you!

He must be heavy. If we make a very tight left turn on the go-around, we *should* miss him, but then we'll lose sight of him...and so close too. That's a fine set of choices. Steady on the glideslope...just a little high now to give us time, keep us off the ground just a little while longer...buy us a little time. We're in ground effect now.

Ten feet.

He'll be off in a second. He'll be off in a second!

There, off. He's off!

Five feet. We're on!

Stay with it, stay with it.

"Wipers on!"

Lightning strike nearby, thunder, visibility drops to almost nothing in the downpour.

"Stay with it, stay with it. There's *our* turn off."

"Prima donnas..."

"Huh?'

"...my old man would say. But I don't think so now."

"What?"

"Nothing."

Choosing Freedom

The Phoenix sky shines brightly through the windows. So bright that the restaurant walls become silhouettes and the booths like the one I am sitting in become darkly private. My body thinks it's lunchtime though the breakfast menu is all that is available.

I am dressed in a flannel shirt and worn jeans and though today is a working day, I have a few hours to kill before I become adrift in that same sky with the blinding sunshine. Restaurants are a keen place to gather thoughts, a cleansing of the mind as I experience regional cuisine from the various places that I go, and the food sort of becomes a point of focusing. They become my own dining room; hotels become my own home when I am away. Though each one is different, they fade into the same place eventually.

The menu is the same—omelet with ham and cheese, pancake, two eggs and hash-brown or home fries, muffin or fruit, orange juice. They throw in their regional or personal touch, which differentiates each place, maybe adding a certain type of salsa or hot sauce, cheeses, or size of muffin, but it's all the same.

"Coffee?"

I transfer my gaze from the window to a thin, black woman with her hair pulled back and a stunning smile.

"Please," I say, and she pours.

"Do you know what you would like?"

Without opening the menu I say, "Ham and cheese omelet, wheat toast, hash browns, thank you." It's a burgeoning heart attack that I know I will regret when I am fifty, but who looks that far ahead?

She scribbles on a pad, smiles again, and walks toward the kitchen.

As I sit alone waiting for my order, uninterested in a crumpled newspaper that I gathered from a vacated booth, I notice a group of people sitting across from me through the outer periphery of my eye. They mumble in hushed tones; a man, who by the peppered waviness of his hair appears wealthy, sitting next to a young professional woman in business attire, perhaps his secretary. They sit across from a large, balding man with sweat trickling down his forehead. I can hear words like, "mergers," "golden parachute," and, "investor basis."

The woman sits quietly, occasionally taking notes and running her index finger through a strand of ebony hair that finds its way into her right eye every few minutes. When the bald man says, "business model," "long term yield," and "half valuation," she focuses on him obligingly, but after a minute I see her glance toward the window at the Saguaro cactus standing at attention up a distant hill. Her "boss" then speaks in turn with, "back end transaction," "seize that ground," "profit margin," and the bald man's pea sized eyes begin to stroll upon the woman's chest and face and then join her wistful daydreaming momentarily. Then the "boss" cut a piece of orange cantaloupe and slowly chews on it until all eyes find him again.

A plate of hot food arrives in my mental absence, placed gently on the table by the woman with the Haitian accent.

"Here you are. Be careful. The plate is very hot."

"Thank you," I say.

"Can I get you anything else?" she says, leaning toward me, her dark eyes radiating congeniality.

"No, this all looks pretty good."

"Very well. Enjoy," she says, and walks away.

As my side of the restaurant reverberates with, "prime equity," "carry back," and "their money is cheaper," I cut the omelet with a fork and chew. The woman scribbles and sighs. The boss drums his fingers on the table, while the bald man clears his throat. There were others here too, other people who don't appear to be doing business, caring for not a word from them. But to me, each "balloon interest," and "large transaction," and corresponding far away look makes me think about my place in the sky. I can't wait to get back to work again.

While they work, they dream; I dream of my work. I dream of a thousand shades of blue on a frosty Denver morning, and of the snow-dusted plains of Nebraska. I know soon I will be flying high above the checkerboard sections and mirrored lakes of Minnesota as we glisten, a tiny speck leading a long contrail line through the sky. I will appreciate the confluence of rivers as only an airman can, and following them as a modern day Lewis and Clark to the far reaches of the Washington coast. I will walk among aluminum wings with little oily streaks, and smell jet exhaust, and hear the sound of breakaway thrust. And I will not think of anything that has to do with "cash flow," and "stabilized purchases," but I will think of "fuel flow," and "stabilized approaches."

I will thank the odds of having a captain whom I have not seen in twenty years, not since before either of us made a living in aviation. For there is nothing more truthful in the airline business than the statement, "It's a Small World," because often a pilot meets another he hasn't seen in so long. And reunions are as significant and stratospheric as finding a long lost relative. To work with him, as I know I will later, is the icing on the cake of what will be a perfect day.

I take a forkful of egg with an equal amount of cheese and ham and fold it onto a piece of toast. I lift it like a shingle to my mouth and bite into it.

I suppose it could have been me sitting over there fretting about leveraging profits and minimizing losses and risks. But no one held a gun to any of our heads when we decided to choose what we wanted to do with our lives. I know that many people, perhaps even those three, balked at the thought of taking a vow of poverty at some young age, faced with the choice of either a life in the heavens or in an office. Could they have done what I, and so many of my fellow pilots, have done? I shake hot sauce over my potatoes. Could they have chosen certain short-term poverty for the opportunity to fly, with no guarantee of steady work or benefits twenty years later?

The owner of my first airline made it clear to us in ground school. He said, "Don't plan on staying here more than two years. Think of this place as a stepping-stone for something else, because I ain't paying you more than $800 a month; and I sure as hell ain't paying any retirement." And we callow birdmen nodded in total agreement. Then when ground school was through for the day, I drove a car that had almost no clutch to a rented trailer that had almost no plumb walls or floor.

How long could the man with the wavy, pepper hair or his dapper secretary have lasted living like that, with no promise of a future more financially rewarding? A pilot's reward is not financial. The reward is freedom from the shackles of the earth, and if we are lucky enough to receive more than $800 a month in the beginning, we count our blessings. At least that is what we do when we first get a taste of professional flying. And though eventually we must accept a fairer wage later on in our profession, the truth becomes evident: Where are we most happy, on the ground or in the air?

The girl catches me staring, and she looks away, disinterested. Worn jeans and a flannel shirt, in an upscale restaurant in Phoenix, no less, I have committed a fashion faux pas once again, thanks to my small overnight bag.

Maybe because of that one time vow of poverty we have a reputation for being cheap, a near epidemic among pilots. Most of us have been there once in the unleveled trailer, and we might be there once again given the insecurity of our profession. Pilots know that prosperity is temporary, furloughs and bankruptcies follow downturns in the economy, and we all retire at sixty whether we are ready or not, provided our hearts hold out.

I slowly push the last quarter of my omelet away, dropping the toast on it.

"Minimum investment,"

"But the long term yield?"

"Hey, we're all players in the market."

I wipe the corners of my mouth and drop the napkin in a wad onto my plate. I drink my coffee. Someone laughs from a dark corner somewhere else in the room.

"Listen, it's all structured."

"The capital is appreciating."

"X-squared."

"What size of fund again?"

"Focus on new technology."

"They have my securities, of course."

The golden parachute they seek sounds more like a lead weight. The riches they seek sound more like shackles.

Soon I will take to the sky.

[END]

0-595-31505-4

Printed in the United States
36644LVS00004B/382-399

9 780595 315055